Expect a Miracle

A Refusal to Give Up

Marianne Jones Hooker

Copyright © 2012 by Marianne Jones Hooker

Published by: Light Books Publishing
1750 Kalakaua Avenue, Suite 103-450
Honolulu, Hawaii 96826 U.S.A.
www.LightBooksPublishing.com

All rights reserved. No part of this book may be reproduced by any mechanical, photographic, or electronic process, or in the form of a phonographic recording; nor may it be stored in a retrieval system, transmitted, or otherwise be copied for public or private use—other than for "fair use" as brief quotations embodied in articles and reviews without prior written permission of the publisher.

Library of Congress Control Number: 2011944453

ISBN: 978-1-4675-0521-5

Editor: Sabrina Rood

Cover Design: Amy O'Donnell

First Published, January 2012

Printed in the United States of America

CONTENTS

Introduction	V
1. Family	11
2. My Family Looked Good but Felt Bad	25
3. The Forbidden Topic—Incest	43
4. Addictions	51
5. Dealing with the Influence of My Heritage	59
6. Symptoms of Sociopaths You Might Overlook	79
7. From Revolving Closet Door to Real Love	91
8. Marriage and Stepparenting	103
9. Drill Sergeant Worked Wonders with My Kids	111
10. The Temporality of Life	121
11. A Refusal to Give Up	129
12. Acknowledging My Angels	149
Sources	158

INTRODUCTION

Writing this book has been both liberating and terrifying. I am afraid I have said too much. I am also afraid I haven't said enough. I was raised not to air my dirty laundry in public, to keep family secrets safe, and to ignore the elephants in the living room, even those pink ones. My grandfather always said everybody has a book in them. When people meet me and hear a little bit about me, they always say that I should write a book. I love to write and have always wanted to write a book, but my story is so disjointed that I didn't know where to start or end. I was afraid of the consequences of disclosing family secrets. I was afraid of being shunned by my family or causing them harm or embarrassment. Both of my parents are now dead. My mother died as I was writing the book. She expressed to her caretakers her concern about my book. Even though my parents are gone and won't know the difference, I do, and I want to honor them and acknowledge the fact that they were doing the very best they could with what they had to work with.

Having counseled many individuals, couples, and families for twenty-three years, I know my story is no worse or better than many others and wondered if I really had something useful to offer to the reader. Then I went to a workshop on self-publishing facilitated by Dr. Zeal and heard him say that nothing is original anymore, that it's all repackaging. I knew then that I could publish this book.

I didn't want to share the story of a drama queen, nor did I seek pity. I am grateful for the life I have lived and the lessons

I have learned because they have enabled me to help others and to be a better person. Everybody experiences trauma in one form or another. It's what we do with it that makes all the difference. I wanted to write a book that will help the reader see that all these adversities of life are but fertilizer for the budding rose. One of my favorite metaphors when working with clients is this: "When you are going through a painful incident, which I call AFGE (another fu*&ing growth experience), you look at it and see that it's brown and lumpy. You say, hmmm, brown and lumpy, must be poop, but on the other side of it, when the pain is gone, you look at it, and you see that it's still brown and lumpy. But you now recognize that it is really chocolate ice cream." Like they say, life is lived forward and understood backwards.

As I edited the first draft of this book, I got bitten by a spider and developed an allergic reaction which caused my eyes to swell. "What is it that I don't want to see?" I asked myself. I studied the spider as totem. In his book, Animal Speak, Ted Andrews says: "Spider (weaving fate), don't take the roundabout way, be straight. Weave something new. Trust feeling rather than seeing."

Spiders' webs can be seen as a metaphor representing the connections among past, present, and future. The spider reminds me not to get caught up in other people's definitions of me, that people have defined the "me" they thought I "should" be from birth on. I am not what others thought I was. The more I tried to be the authentic me that I was born to be, the more I was labeled as a rebel, a black sheep, or just plain crazy.

I got locked into trying to be what others wanted me to be, a false self, because they were my authority figures and it kept me in my comfort zone. The fears of the unknown kept me there. It is far easier to live in the hell I know than to risk discovering that there is another way which may be better for me. To me this false self that many of us take on to please the authorities in our lives is at the root of all "mental illness." Self-worth is about taking calculated risks.

Every time I see a spider weaving its web I pause and admire its beauty and perfection and the infinite possibilities within its web. In writing this book, it is my hope that I am achieving just what the spider wanted—helping others recognize their magnificence and infinite potential!

The most important message that I hope you get from my book is to not give up before the miracles start happening in your own life, and if you live your life expecting the miracles, they will eventually come. The miracles could be already happening and you just haven't acknowledged, accepted, or allowed them. Life can be hard, no doubt, but if you can't change the exterior, change your thoughts and perceptions. That will change everything. Choose thoughts that make you feel good and eliminate those that don't. You have control over your happiness and your reality by controlling your thoughts. While I was growing up, my father had a plaque on his desk that read, "The problem is not the problem; the problem is what you think about the problem." I agree with that. If I'm able to see a problem as an opportunity or a challenge, I get excited. I vibrate at a more positive level. But if I see it as complicated, or as something to be endured, then, of course, my enthusiasm diminishes and I feel discouraged. As my husband frequently reminds me, I get to choose what kind of day I want to have.

Always look for the blessings, the synchronicities, and the miracles, however small. Wake up each morning with a list of all the things you are grateful for and you'll see them multiply. Jump out of bed each day with the wonder and awe of a child, with excitement and anticipation about what the new day holds for you!

Some of the names in this book have been changed to protect the privacy of the individuals involved.

One

Family

"IF YOU MEET A WOMAN OF WHATEVER COMPLEXION who sails her life with strength and grace and assurance, talk to her! And what you will find is that there has been a suffering, that at some time she has left herself for hanging dead."

— SENA JETER NASLUND

I was born and raised in Pine Bluff, Arkansas. Back in my day, it was a safe place. I rode my bike all around town, anywhere I wanted to go. It wasn't a bad place to grow up except that there was, and still is today, a large gap between the haves and the have-nots. Pine Box, some folks call it today because nobody wants to live there. It's a place to come and die. It was once a bustling riverfront agricultural community but with the way things are now, it has the highest crime rate per capita of any town in the United States. Crime Bluff, I call it. It has a paper mill on either side of town, so it stinks anywhere you are. The population is predominantly black now and many of them are really poor. Many of the young people are heavily into drugs, gang activity, and crime. Most who can, have moved away. People can barely give away their property let alone sell it, although there are still a lot of lovely homes there.

Forty-five miles southeast of Little Rock and a hundred years back was my family home. Supper was served at 5:30 p.m. every day, at precisely thirty minutes after Daddy got home from work. Protocol was strict. If one of us kids was a minute late to the table, he or she didn't get to eat.

I have three older brothers. My oldest is Bill, ten years older, then Bubba, eight years older, and Stuart, four years my senior. Daddy was the ruler of the table. We sat at a long picnic table with hard benches on each side. My parents sat at each end in comfy chairs with armrests. I sat between Mama and my oldest brother, Bill, "the shoveler." My brother Bubba sat across from me and my other brother, Stuart, sat across from Bill. Our maid, Faithie, usually stood behind us in the kitchen, always ready to serve if we needed anything. My parents made her eat in the kitchen and I hated that because I loved her. I thought of her as a member of my family and felt closer to her than most members of my own family.

Stuart usually acted up and got sent to the pantry to eat. If he was still obnoxious, my father would send him to his room in the back of the house. Stuart would go into the bathroom and start hocking lugies (phlegm) to make us lose our appetites. It didn't bother anybody but me. I would holler at Mama, "Please make him stop!" Of course the problem was always mine. My father would say, "I- G- N- O- R- E," and I would get so frustrated because I couldn't spell. Once I got older and understood what he meant, I would say, "I can't!" That would end supper for me.

My brothers were pretty rowdy at the table. Food was great but controlled. My mama was a gourmet cook but she always had me on a diet. This was confusing to me, considering that every time Mama got mad at Daddy, she would eat a half gallon of old-fashioned peach ice cream all by herself. I would always beg her for a spoonful but she wouldn't share. Because of that, to this day, I don't like ice cream or anything peach. Our meals consisted of carefully selected choices from the four major food groups. We didn't eat anything Daddy didn't like, which included most of my favorite foods. The house always smelled good because of Mama's cooking—I always enjoyed coming home to the smells of freshly baked bread or fried bacon.

Faithie did all the work in the kitchen while Mama kept busy supervising. Faithie always made my tea just the way I liked it. When my parents sent me to the mental institution in North Carolina at age sixteen, I had to learn to make my own tea because all the ready-made tea they had was "sweet tea." Yuck! Faithie knew the right amount of lemon and sweetener to add. Faithie provided most of the love in our house. She always called me "May-Anne" because she couldn't pronounce her Rs. If we were having "swimps," as she called them, for supper, she and I would stand side by side over the double stainless steel kitchen sink and peel and devein them with bottle openers and pecan picks. I always snuck a few to eat before Mama put them in the remoulade sauce because the Zatarin's creole mustard was too spicy for me. I always teased Faithie and tried to get her to try a shrimp. She would say, "Oooo weeee, no way, Miss May-Anne. I use swimps for bait when I go fishing!" We would laugh those deep wonderful belly laughs together. Even now, I love to cook, peel, devein, and eat jumbo shrimp, although I'm not convinced deveining is necessary.

We called my brother Bill "Dooner" because he couldn't say Bill Jones, Jr. He would say, "Bill Done Dooner." He had a hollow leg so we all wanted to get served before he got his. He can easily bankrupt an all-you-can-eat buffet restaurant! When I was nineteen, I was really overweight and teased regularly by my siblings and peers until I had my stomach stapled, both of which helped me lose 150 pounds. My brother Bill used to say that I was his half sister, that we were the Goodrich family, the family without the blimp. If we were having steak with a marinade, he would say, "Marianne-ade-it-all."

Bill taught me how to make rice with butter and sugar—yummy comfort food! He's got integrity and was Daddy's shining star. My daddy passed away over four years ago and my mom just passed away in September 2011, as this book was being written. She died on the tenth anniversary of 9/11. Just like Mama to go out with a bang! Bubba and Stuart live in Pine Bluff and Bill lives in Little Rock. Bill is now a CPA and a financial planner and he did a wonderful job taking care of Mama's finances and protecting her from my greedy brother. When she was in the nursing home, he tended to her the most, right up until her final days. He took her shopping and out to lunch. I really appreciate him. Stuart works a lot and has a long commute to work; he saw Mom whenever he could, really stepping up to the plate in her final days when he realized he was needed. When Daddy died he wanted Mama to have around-the-clock care, for he knew how dangerous she was alone. About fifteen years before Daddy died, Mama had a cerebral aneurysm but survived. Daddy became her full-time devoted caretaker. As she aged, she said she wanted to go to the nursing home in Pine Bluff and my brothers wanted her there. I wanted her with me, but majority ruled. I knew I would have taken better care of her than my brothers could, but the vote was in their favor.

My brother Bill has had the same girlfriend for fifteen years and won't make her legal, something that's really important to her. I don't know why she puts up with him. Bill's only child is in prison for a long time and I think that breaks his heart. That's why he eats so much and has become closed hearted. He had a head injury in college, which devastated my father. Bill has not been socially right since. He is a brilliant, handsome, and honest man. He's so smart that he became a master bridge player in one year. He spends most of his time working out and playing bridge. He only talks after he's had a few drinks. I hate it every time he quits drinking. I miss him. He almost died about ten years ago from sarcoma but he's doing well now. I am so glad he made it. Without him, I couldn't have made it through all the family drama that followed my daddy's death. I loved my daddy. He protected me from my older brothers. When he died, I lost my protector.

We never had booze at the table. My parents quit drinking to raise the kids. We had orange juice at breakfast, tea at lunch, and water at supper. Mama didn't want us to have caffeine in our system so close to bedtime. We had to make a happy plate before we could eat dessert. Since I was usually on a diet, I had to sit and watch them eat the sweet stuff most of the time. When we were excused from the table and everybody else went to bed, I would sneak into the kitchen and help myself.

There were a number of advantages in being a part of my family. We were well known. I am the great-great-niece of the first carpetbagger governor of Arkansas. His brother was the prosecuting attorney and helped hanging Judge Parker create his court in Fort Smith, Arkansas. That's what the movie True Grit is about. His brother was a senator, and that was my great-grandfather. A book called Who Killed John Clayton? was written about him. All three brothers were assassinated. I was part of the fifth generation of our family in this small town. My family was well established in Pine Bluff and we had status. I was known either as my brothers' little sister or as my parents' daughter. So the road was pretty well paved for me as a child. My father, Bill Jones, was a farmer and a John Deere tractor dealer. When I was in grade school he patented a cultivator which made him very successful. My mother, Betty, was a housewife. She worked as a secretary before she married my father.

The most influential people in my life when I was growing up were all black: our maid, Faithie, our babysitter, Willie Lewis, and our caterer, Hortense Jones. They had the most positive influence on me. I was born with a very tender heart and so much compassion. I hated seeing them live in poverty. There was such a vast contrast between our lifestyle and theirs. We lived in a huge, elaborately decorated house with all the amenities you can imagine, while the blacks lived in shanties. As kids, we used to call our living room The Museum because it was so fancy, and we weren't allowed to go in there except for weddings, funerals, and parties. I was ashamed of our affluence, although we weren't showy or extravagant like other rich people in town. It was the contrast that bothered me. I felt guilty and wanted to give away everything. I'd gift clothes to our maid and babysitter, but Mother didn't want me giving away too much. I'd give them everything I could give them, including my love and devotion.

The internationally famous crisis at Central High School in Little Rock happened the year after my birth. The Supreme Court ruled in 1954 that racial desegregation in public schools violated the Fourteenth Amendment to the Constitution. Public schools began to tackle how to develop a plan that would be successful. The original plan was gradual and incremental. However, the Supreme Court issued its decision and directed the schools to desegregate with "all deliberate speed." The issues were returned to federal courts for implementation of the new decision. The year I was born, the NAACP (National Association for the Advancement of Colored People) sued the Little Rock School District. To make a long story short, the federal government trumped the governor of Arkansas, Orville Faubus, and literally forced nine black students into Central High with the National Guard at their side. There was much resistance to desegregation, racial tensions were high, and the Civil Rights movement had begun.

Integration of schools in my hometown happened when I

Expect a Miracle

left elementary school and started seventh grade, a challenging enough transition without the added stress of dealing with the racial tensions and a totally new way of schooling. It was in the seventh grade that I had my first bad encounter with a black woman. She was my math teacher and had a chip on her shoulder. She was cruel and abusive. I was shocked. She hit my hands with a ruler more times than I can count and had me stand in the corner over and over, arms extended, with heavy text books in each arm and one leg bent off the floor. I don't know how long I had to stand there— it was usually in response to me talking during class—but it felt like forever. I was ashamed and humiliated, flunked math, and began to hate it.

I began to develop friendships with the black girls at school. They were more fun to me than many of the white girls. I couldn't understand why I couldn't bring them to my house or go to theirs when Faithie was there every day, our gardener was black, as were so many of our babysitters and some of our employees at the family business. My father and I had heated conversations about it but he always won.

I learned that skin color means absolutely nothing about who a person is. I have been repelled by racism and bigotry since birth. It's the soul and how you express it that's important. I lived in a family that looked good and felt bad. They lived in families that looked bad and felt good. The people whom I witnessed living "The American Dream" on the outside were often living "The American Nightmare" behind closed doors. In my hometown blacks were forced to live in shanties and many had Coke machines on their front porches to supplement their income. They had to live and stay in "colored town" unless they were coming to work for the white people as maids, gardeners, or butlers. Faithie didn't have the opportunity to drive until I was probably in high school. I will always remember the first time she drove up to work in her little green car. She parked in our driveway and got out of her car in her white uniform and apron. She was so proud of herself and I was so proud of her, too! She had worked long and hard to study for her driver's license, learn to drive, and buy herself a car!

If I needed someone to talk to, Faithie was there; if I got in trouble at school, which happened pretty frequently, she would come get me; if I got sick at school, she would be the one to come get me. She was the one to pull my boots off after playing in the snow and serve me a cup of hot chocolate with marshmallows on top. When Faithie got cancer I went to see her in the hospital. I was so glad to see her but so sad to see her so sick. I knew she was near the end and I had to rush out to keep from totally breaking down in her hospital room. My parents didn't tell me she died until after her funeral, so I didn't get to go. That hurt me so much and made me so upset with my parents. After Faithie died, I kept in touch with her daughter, Modenia, for many years but we have lost contact. I pray for her and wish her well. I know she knows how much I love her mama and how much I appreciate her sharing her mama with me. What she probably doesn't know is how jealous I was of her and her siblings when I was growing up because she got to stay with Faithie when I had to go back home to the white side of town.

Expect a Miracle

My father was in the Navy during WWII and was at Pearl Harbor on VJ Day, Victory over Japan, the day Japan surrendered. He hated the Japanese. He acted like he hated blacks too, because that's what a white man was supposed to do in the South in those days. He hated Jews, Chinese, and Mexicans. Well, that's what he always said, whether or not he actually meant it. I don't think that deep inside himself he really felt like that. I think his heart was so tender he didn't know how to deal with it and resorted to looking tough. He loved to get a rise out of people. Mama would go, "Honey don't talk like that," and I would say, "Daddy, stop!"

Daddy didn't like the smell of fish cooking, so we didn't eat it. Daddy didn't like the smell of cabbage, so we didn't have it in the house. His grandmother had raised him and he was a silver spoon boy right from the start. He was an only child until his little sister, Ann, came along when he was sixteen. If little Billy didn't want to eat his peas he didn't have to. Mother ran the whole ship around him and what he wanted to do. Whatever he said, we all went along with it. Both my parents were Scorpios so I know there was a lot of emotion and passion there but neither showed it in front of me. Mama was very intelligent, very capable. She took care of all the books for the family. She was very involved in charity work and civic organizations. She wanted to go to college but her parents couldn't afford to send her.

Mother raised us right. We were expected to be well mannered, know which fork and knife to use, put our napkin on our lap first, and so on. She was so concerned about looking good that she would consult a book of etiquette by Amy Vanderbilt or Emily Post for every situation. My brother Bill didn't think as highly of Amy Vanderbilt as did my mother. Amy Vanderbilt was rumored to have committed suicide, falling to her death from a second-floor window. My brother therefore dismissed her as an authority in etiquette, saying that committing suicide wasn't very good etiquette.

When I was five, my parents had a party and all of their friends came over for dinner. As they started pouring the drinks, my mother's friend Marthann noticed her drink tasted strange. She wondered if the 7UP was flat and proceeded to pass it around for everyone to taste. My oldest brother, Bill, slipped in the room and told my mother that my brother Bubba had tee-teed (urinated) into the 7UP bottle. What Bill didn't say was that he encouraged Bubba to pee into the bottle after he poured out some of the 7UP.

When Willie moved to Hot Springs, Mama retained elderly white babysitters. The first few were wonderful and provided much love, similar to the black ladies. Then came Mrs. Brewer! She would just talk, talk, and talk and was so incredibly boring. But she did have a salt and pepper shaker collection that I admired. I always wanted to collect something but never could decide what. By this time, my brothers were teenagers and didn't want anything to do with me. I felt so alone.

One day when Mrs. Brewer came to babysit me, I was in the living room watching TV when I noticed it had gotten awfully quiet in the back of the house where Stuart and Bubba were supposed to be. I went to the back of the house looking for my brothers and they weren't there, but the window was open. I went and told the babysitter they weren't there. One of my brothers had stolen my parents' car and was out driving around. When Bubba drove back into the driveway from his joy ride, he turned off the headlights and attempted to get back into the house unnoticed. But he saw headlights coming down the other side of the driveway. He was scared shitless thinking they had been caught by my parents. But it was the babysitter's car. And who was behind the wheel? My brother Stuart! I told on them because I was mad they didn't take me along with them. My two oldest brothers were crazy with each other. They fought a lot, and they still fight. Bill broke Bubba's nose on one occasion while practicing karate; I don't think it was intentional. Bill picked on Bubba, who in turn picked on Stuart, and both Bubba and Stuart picked on me. At various times each brother was my hero, Stuart most often. Oftentimes they were outright abusive. Sibling abuse is just as damaging as parental abuse. Bubba was psychologically abusive to me until I was in my twenties.

One Easter, when I was four, my family had an Easter egg hunt. My mother's friend JoAnne had painted a golden egg for Bubba which was included in the hunt. Bubba was eleven at the time. I found the golden egg in the hunt and my mother attempted to pry it out of my hands to give back to Bubba. My four-year-old brain thought that since I found it, the egg was mine. I looked at Bubba, looked at my parents, and then ran and smashed the egg on the street. That became a favorite family story for many years to come. They claimed that on that day, it became evident that Marianne was possessed by the devil.

Although they were half teasing, the behavior was a source of shame to me for most of my life—until I met my husband, Bill. I was almost fifty years old when I told Bill the story: he was surprised that my parents made such a big deal out of it. Not only that, he was curious why an eleven-year-old boy—my brother—would want to hunt Easter eggs with his four-year-old little sister.

Bubba's abuse stopped temporarily when I was a young adult when my beloved grandmother threatened to disinherit him if he didn't stop. His behavior toward me became much nastier after Daddy died. I suppose he was jealous because Bill was Daddy's number one star and the smartest, and I was the youngest and only girl. He didn't have any way to find recognition within the family unit.

Two

My Family Looked Good but Felt Bad

"Life will break you. Nobody can protect you from that, and living alone won't either, for solitude will also break you with its yearning. You have to love. You have to feel. It is the reason you are here on earth. You are here to risk your heart."

— Louise Erdrich

My Family Looked Good but Felt Bad

Have you ever envied a certain family that you know? Well, you may have to think again. Some families look great on the outside: they are rich, appear happy, and seem to have everything under control. On closer look, however, it's all a façade. My family had money, no doubt, but all the other appearances were just that, appearances! We have mental illness and alcohol abuse on both sides of the family, but they seemed to prefer the diagnosis of mental illness. They probably didn't mind being mentally ill because they wanted to be able to drink.

But in my opinion, as I stated in the introduction, mental illness develops when people suppress their true souls for whatever reason. Alcohol is often the lubrication that allows people to get through that suppression of self. I come from a long line of interesting characters who could not possibly be themselves in the South. They were nuts by the standards and expectations of the times! My parents' exposure to therapy was when they dropped off my brother and me to our psychiatrists' offices or sat in on our sessions. I have often wondered not only why my parents didn't get help but why they chose not to get help for my two oldest brothers.

My parents had major issues of their own, but they chose to either deny or live with them. My maternal grandfather was an alcoholic, and my paternal grandfather and grandmother enjoyed their booze, too. On both sides there was the diagnosis of manic depression; the treatments included hospitalization and shock treatments. My much-beloved grandmother, Thelma, who we called "Mamaw," came from eastern Kentucky, a town called Cross the Creek from Hell for Certain.

Although my father turned out to become a very successful businessman, he did horribly in school. My son was diagnosed with attention-deficit/hyperactivity disorder (ADHD) at age six, and I have often wondered if my father and son had similar issues. My son was put on medications and became violent, often chasing me with knives. In sixth grade, he was later diagnosed with an autism spectrum disorder, nonverbal learning disorder. In reality I think he was just walking to the beat of his own drummer. I must admit, however, that throughout his development he was really immature for his age.

My dad's friend Adam Robinson owned a funeral home. When he and my dad were kids, they threw cats off the roof. I've seen my father be cruel to animals. He loved dogs, but I've seen him pick at them until they became very uncomfortable. He had a cruel streak to him at times and no respect for boundaries. Many times he would help himself to food on my plate and laugh when I got upset. My grandmother was a wonderful person, but she had terrible mood swings. She would get way too up or way too low. She often embarrassed me while on her highs because she said whatever was on her mind without restraint. Her brother was a psychiatrist and was the head of the state hospital in Little Rock. He'd go crazy every now and then and have to go to Connecticut to The Institute for Living and get stabilized through medication. He and my maternal grandmother were both diagnosed as manic depressive (bipolar, it's called today), so I think it made it easy for my psychiatrist to slap the label cyclothymic on me.

So, yeah, there was a lot of mental illness in my family. My great-uncle committed suicide and my great-grandfather who was a judge once fell down on the courthouse steps, drunk! My great-grandfather was an excellent swimmer yet he drowned in a lake, and the family has always wondered if he committed suicide. My great-uncle died by shooting himself.

In spite of their mental problems my ancestors held positions of high esteem in the community. I ask myself how they got there. I don't think it was as a result of their education but more a result of the kind of people they were, salt of the earth, people with character, trying to do the right thing, and giving more than taking. I suspect people overlooked their eccentricities.

Despite being the black sheep and the "crazy one," I think I've been the most successful member of my family. My brothers worked for my dad. When my father sold the John Deere dealerships, it was with the stipulation that they keep my brother Stuart on board. My brother Bubba appointed himself general manager of our manufacturing business long ago, dug his heels in, and refused to leave. He has terrorized everybody in the family, including my parents. I'm the only one with a master's degree, successful in a career independent of the family, and the only one to move away. My brothers might disagree with my opinions and probably do, and that's okay. Despite all my personal and professional accomplishments, I think both of my parents died not really seeing me for who I am, but for the girl I was as a teenager. My hope is that they can see the real me from the other side, and with them and their control of me gone from this plane I will continue to step up to the plate to be my true self.

In and Out of Mental Institutions for Ten Years

When I was fourteen, I started acting out, starved for attention and a silent sufferer of incest. All my brothers had left home and I was stuck with my parents. I started drinking, smoking, and cursing. I sucked my thumb from birth until I was eleven. My mother didn't like that and tried many things to stop me to no avail and finally got my pediatrician to put a large brace on it so I couldn't get it in my mouth. My parents kept cigarettes on the dining room table and I went straight from sucking my thumb to smoking cigarettes.

I went to church campouts and did stupid stuff for attention, like cursing out the preacher's son and swimming in a freezing cold lake in late fall. I also took an overdose of aspirin and went to Youth Group and told them I had overdosed. I was already getting heavy, probably weighing close to 200 pounds. I had bad acne and an underactive thyroid, and I was making regular trips to the "fat doctor," who prescribed amphetamines and put me on a variety of diets.

First my parents sent me to my pediatrician and I wouldn't open up to him; after all, I was a teenager, not a child. Then they sent me to our preacher, Brother Ed. He was like a father to me and still is to this day. His wife was like a mother to me. I opened up somewhat to Brother Ed, but I never talked to him about what was really at the root of my problems—incest. After a series of visits, he said he couldn't do anything else, so my mother consulted my uncle, who was the administrator of the Arkansas State Hospital. He referred me to a psychiatrist. At this point my brother was also seeing a psychiatrist. He got mixed up with drugs in college, went to our preacher's house for help, and that's how my parents found out. They arranged to get him admitted to the psych ward. When I visited my brother there, I liked it so much that I wanted to be admitted, too. So I started acting out more and more.

Expect a Miracle

When I was in the tenth grade in a private school, I craved the attention of my math teacher. Everyone else hated her, but I loved her. Like my father, I couldn't bare my tender heart and say I wanted attention, so I recruited a friend and we let the air out of the teacher's car tires. Well, I got lots of attention for that! I became the first girl to be suspended from that school. Following my suspension, my doctor put me on heavy doses of medication: antidepressants when I was sad, tranquilizers when I was happy or out of control, and lithium at all times.

My parents and the psychiatrist agreed that I needed hospitalization, so they admitted me to the psychiatric ward at St. Vincent in Little Rock. Pine Bluff didn't have a psych ward, otherwise I would have gone there. I was at St. Vincent for six weeks, and the doctor had me on "no demand" status, which meant short of hurting myself or others, they let me do whatever I wanted to do so they could watch and observe me. I took advantage of the freedom in the ward and after six weeks my shrink said he had done all he could do for me, that I needed a higher level of care. What rebellious teenager wouldn't have taken advantage of the freedom?

My parents gave me a choice of mental institutions in three different states: Connecticut, North Carolina, and Texas. In Texas institutionalized kids were sent to school at the local public schools. I didn't want to ride the "short bus" (the bus normally used for special needs kids, easily identifiable as it is shorter than a normal school bus) from the mental institution to school with all the "normies." Connecticut was too far away. But the mental institution in North Carolina had a high school on campus and the man who would be my doctor was friends with my doctor in Arkansas. I liked having connections.

My mother had tried to get me into Miss Hockaday's School for Girls in Dallas but they didn't have uniforms big enough to fit me. I was already a size 18 and was putting on more weight fast. I was heavily medicated, and I think that was contributing to the weight gain. I'd come home after school and sleep all afternoon. Many afternoons I would go to Debra's house. She was my best friend. Her parents were my surrogate parents, and her sister, "Boney," as we called her, is "my sister from a different mister" to this day. I felt comfortable at their house. Debra's mom was real like I was, and what you saw was what you got. Not at my house. I know I wouldn't be alive today without the Westbrooks, Debra's family. They loved me, spent time with me, and gave me hope for a brighter day. They never talked bad about my family, and my parents appreciated them.

I took off to Asheville, North Carolina, to Highland Hospital, Duke University's long-term psychiatric division. It had been a health sanatorium before Duke University took it over. Later Duke sold it to a large corporation. Highland Hospital, originally known as "Dr. Carroll's Sanatorium," was founded by Dr. Robert S. Carroll, a distinguished psychiatrist. His treatment program for mental disorders and addictions was based on exercise, diet, and occupational therapy. The facility attracted patients from all over the country. The hospital relocated from downtown Asheville to the northern end of Montford Avenue in 1909 and was officially named Highland Hospital in 1912.

The campus included landscaped grounds to help patients

recover by means of "diversion" and "productive occupation." A variety of Georgian Colonial style buildings housed the patients. The campus included Dr. Carroll's home at 19 Zillicoa Street, known as Homewood. Dr. Carroll's wife, world-renowned concert pianist Grace Potter Carroll, operated a music school in their house where she gave lessons and held performances for many years. Among her students was Nina Simone, a nationally known jazz musician. In 1939, Dr. Carroll entrusted the hospital to the Neuropsychiatric Department of Duke University. Tragically, on the night of March 10, 1948, a deadly fire broke out in the main building and took the lives of nine women. Among the victims was author Zelda Fitzgerald, wife of F. Scott Fitzgerald. Duke University owned the property until the 1980s. Today the complex has been converted to an industrial office park and a shopping plaza.

I was at Highland Hospital for eight months the first time. By this time, I was considered institutionalized, meaning that I couldn't function in the free world. I'd come back home to Arkansas and end up checking into local psychiatric wards there. I remember the first time I came home from the mental institution after eight months there. I was so excited to be set free and looked forward to a normal life with my family. It was the style among my peers to buy our clothes at thrift stores. I had bought a special dress for the occasion and couldn't wait to see my parents and friends to show them how much I had changed. When I got off the plane my mother was horrified at my attire; I guess she didn't think I looked so good.

Love was a word never spoken in our family and I came home with plans to change that. The first thing I said to both parents was how much I missed and loved them. They did not respond. Not long before my mother died, I was visiting her in the nursing home when my brother and sister-in-law came to see her. When they left, they told her they loved her. She responded, "I love you, too." She then turned and looked at me and said, "You started all of that."

It turned out that I was in and out of Highland Hospital for ten years. I graduated from high school on the campus of Highland Hospital. I was one of five graduating students. My diploma says Asheville High School but it's actually from a mental institution. Once I graduated from high school, I tried to go to college back in Arkansas by applying there. I got accepted to Hendrix College, an excellent Methodist school in a dry county of Arkansas. A dry county is a county where you can't legally buy alcohol. I enrolled in Hendrix and went through the four days of orientation. Unfortunately, I spent the entire time buying and drinking liquor, trying to cope with the realities of the free world. On the fifth day of orientation, which was the first day of classes, I dropped out. I went to stay with our minister, Brother Ed, and his wife, Pat, for a little while. As I was writing this book I wanted outside perspectives of me and wrote to many outside friends for their views of me. I got back a lot of responses; most were glowing and more useful for the marketing of the book. This was Brother Ed's reply:

Expect a Miracle

REFLECTIONS ON A 40-YEAR FRIENDSHIP

It was in mid-1970 that my family moved to Pine Bluff, AR, the newly appointed pastor at Lakeside United Methodist Church, the home church of Marianne's family. She was in junior high, a very active participant in the church's youth ministry. (--and when I say "active" that might be something of an understatement.)

Immediately upon meeting Marianne in those years one is aware of her active, yea, aggressive, always very friendly and, caring nature -- a very intelligent young lady. As we became friends it was apparent that she had some behavioral issues, as though crying out for attention, for the need to harness that energy, that intelligence, that vivacious personality. I shall always appreciate the openness/willingness of her parents -- who likewise became such dear friends --to accept the reality of her situation, and eager to seek the professional help Marianne needed -- which became a rather lengthy, up-and-down journey for all.

In it all Marianne allowed my wife Pat and me to be her trusted friend. And across these 40 years that relationship has remained strong. We have shared in her troubled relationship with her brothers, her romances, marriages and birth and rearing of her children, along with her career choice, training and experiences -- a relationship extending into the illness and death of her dear, kind father and now with concerns for her aging, sweet mother.

It's that "career choice" that bespeaks for me who Marianne really is -- a career that would allow her to seek avenues by which she could care and show concern for others -- always willing to give one the shirt off her back (-albeit she might tell you how to wear it!) -- the desire to assist especially those experiencing anxiety provoking situations, reaching out to them in a uniquely caring, enabling manner.

Rev. Ed Matthews
Aug. 1, 2011

After a week's stay with Brother Ed and Pat, I returned to Little Rock, Arkansas to see a new doctor. The man was hot! I had a big time crush on him. I loved going to therapy with him. He was into this new kind of therapy called Reparenting, where the patient is regressed to infancy and walked through past trauma and abuse, reparented, and brought back again to the present. The late Jacqui Schiff wrote a book about it called All My Children. They were primarily using reparenting for schizophrenics. My new doctor moved me into his house where he was living with his girlfriend and his teenaged son to try it himself. Big mistake! It didn't work. I was jealous of the girlfriend, and I taught his son new bad behaviors like how to get drunk and how to do psychedelic mushrooms in a milkshake format during group therapy.

Not surprising, the doctor labeled me "chronically mentally ill" and recommended that I go to Oakland, California and work with the top specialist, Jacqui Schiff herself, at the Cathexis Institute. Psychotherapy was just coming out of the closet and the treatment of mental illness was in its infancy. Reparenting was controversial at best, abusive and dangerous at worst. I was sent to the program with an anorexic named Gail. She weighed probably 75 pounds soaking wet. She wanted to drive nonstop to California, stopping only to vomit. I, on the other hand, always wanted to stop and eat. Anorexics often starve and vomit. I was a compulsive overeater and all I wanted to do was eat, but we were in her car and she was in control. What a team we were!

When we got to Oakland she abandoned me in a hotel next to a strip joint and an adult bookstore, in the inner city, and took off to see some friends of hers. I had three days before my intake at the Cathexis Institute and I remember being terrified to go out of the room. When I did go for the intake I was horrified by what I saw. In the treatment rooms were adults lying around in diapers, held by staff members who were feeding them milk from baby bottles. While a part of me yearned for the nurturing, a bigger part of me knew that something was badly wrong with this picture. As soon as I had an opportunity, I left and went to a pay phone to call Dr. Bonner at Highland Hospital to see if I could return there. He didn't answer, so I left a message for him to call me at the Cathexis Institute. By the next day he still hadn't called and I began to panic. This was not like him at all. He had always been there for me. I snuck away and called again and he answered and said he had left a message for me at the Institute; they denied it. We agreed that I would return to North Carolina and I got on a red eye out of San Francisco that night. I later learned that Jacqui Schiff had her own psychological problems—she had unfulfilled mothering needs—that motivated her to build a practice. It has been my experience that many therapists go into the field to meet their own needs rather than the needs of their clients, even if unconsciously, and it behooves parents and guardians to do a thorough investigation before choosing a treatment center and making a treatment choice for their loved ones.

As far as psychiatric treatment goes, from my experience, Highland Hospital was better than most. I was there from 1972 to 1982, off and on. There were a lot of good times mixed with lots of insanity. On weekends, we got a chance to go on outings. There was another mental institution on the other side of town and our favorite pastime was to ride by and gawk and laugh at their patients who were wandering about on the lawn. Of course, when tourists rode down our street and gawked at us, we didn't like that. We would put on a show for them by acting like we were really nuts. Most of my fellow patients weren't severe; they were just what we called the "walking wounded."

I would try to leave the hospital but my parents would threaten me, even though I was beyond the age for legal commitment. They would say to me, "If you leave and have problems we'll put you in the state hospital." Well, I had seen the movie One Flew Over the Cuckoo's Nest, and I sure didn't want to go to a state's hospital. So I yielded and allowed them to control me. In fact, my parents also wanted to commit one of my brothers to the same hospital. They sent my brother there for evaluation, and to their surprise, the hospital sent him right back to them with a note saying that he was fine.

I decided to enroll in college in North Carolina. It took me ten years, but I graduated from college. By the time I graduated, I had straightened out considerably. I was free to leave the Institute and was never again hospitalized. But I did continue to see other private medical practitioners and specialists.

Interestingly enough, there were a lot of famous people, whose names I will not mention, who were in the psychiatric hospital. Some were suffering from schizophrenia. I smoked pot with one of them on the front lawn. There was another famous entrepreneur who was served scotch and water every night after dinner, otherwise, he couldn't sleep. To ordinary, non-celebrity patients, the hospital could be oppressive at times. If I didn't do what they said, for example, they would give me a shot and lock me up, or put me in seclusion. It was another type of control. But at the same time, I got a lot of love there. I had nurses who loved me and I had doctors who were good to me. I got more love there than I probably would have gotten at home.

There were also times of great uncertainty. By this time, I was acquainted with a variety of mental conditions and could understand them to some degree. But I had a difficult time understanding a new mental illness that I encountered at the hospital—schizophrenia. Some of the patients whom I lived with were paranoid schizophrenics. All of a sudden, they'd go off and just turn on you for no apparent reason. Here I am, an impressionable youth, and I'm hardly mentally ill, compared to some other patients. Then one of my friends would come speeding toward me and screaming, "I'm gonna kill you," or "The barn is burning." It was hard to understand because they acted in all seriousness, yet, there was no "barn" burning. In fact, there was no barn. Nobody offered an explanation to me for this illness, including the staff.

I remember a ten-year-old young black girl being brought into the psychiatric ward. She had been chained in the woods her whole life and raised like an animal. She ate with her hands. Her parents hadn't wanted anything to do with her. She was brought to the "nut house" to learn how to be social. There were some really crazy people there. Most of them looked no different than you and me; they just had serious stuff going on in their minds. Many people don't know that crazy people like these exist in our society. That's because they're out of sight and not a part of everyday experience. When a person who is living in our free society gets an opportunity to experience the world of our mentally ill citizens, I think that person would walk away with a whole new perspective on life. At the very least, he or she will feel pretty grateful for being somewhat normal.

Schizophrenia is a chronic, severe, debilitating mental illness that affects about one percent of the population, corresponding to more than two million people in the United States alone. Other statistics about schizophrenia indicate that it affects men about one and a half times more commonly than women. It is one of the psychotic mental disorders and is characterized by symptoms of thought, behavior, and social problems. The thought problems associated with schizophrenia are described as psychosis, in which the person's thinking is completely out of touch with reality at times. For example, the sufferer may hear voices or see people that are in no way present or feel like bugs are crawling on their skin when there are none. The individual with this disorder may also have disorganized speech, disorganized behavior, physically rigid or lax behavior (catatonia), significantly decreased behaviors or feelings, as well as delusions, which are ideas about themselves or others that have no basis in reality. For example, they may be paranoid that others are plotting against them when they are not.

At the time I was at the ward in North Carolina, psychiatry was just becoming more accepted and people wanted to know more about it. New drugs were being developed. In fact, I was the first person in Arkansas put on lithium. Doctors thought the drug would fix everything, but it was just another manipulative ploy by the pharmaceutical companies to control people and take their money.

Three

The Forbidden Topic—Incest

"BE AN ADVOCATE FOR FORGIVENESS. It's a powerful weapon... it liberates the soul, USE it!"

— MARIANNE JONES HOOKER

The term incest refers to sex between people of close blood relationship, members of the same household, step-relatives, those related by adoption or marriage, and members of the same clan or lineage. It is illegal in the jurisdiction where it takes place and is considered taboo by different societies around the world. Father-daughter incest was for many years the most commonly reported and studied form of incest. More recently, research shows that sibling incest, particularly older brothers having sexual relations with younger siblings, is the most common form of incest. I experienced incest for four years without my parents' knowledge.

The perpetrator got me to comply by holding a note over my

head that I had written to a classmate with a four-letter-word in it that had gotten into his hands. He threatened to show the note to my parents if I didn't comply. I was so scared of my parents that I gave in each time. It's interesting to me now that I chose to receive horrific abuse for years over the chance of my parents knowing I had written a nasty note. I wanted to say, "Go ahead and show it to them." But I didn't. Instead, I said, "Do what you want." He'd say, "Take off your clothes and lie face down on my bed." That was when I learned to astral travel, the ability to project out of the physical body and explore the psychic and spiritual planes. My little nine-year-old body would lie on top of his rumpled tan chenille bedspread while he got on my back and said he was going to corn-hole me. I didn't even know what that meant but he explained it to me like a childhood game. By the time I returned to my body, he would be done. It's nice that there is a special name for familial sexual abuse, incest. They softened the blow by not calling it what it is: RAPE!

My parents thought I was manic depressive like the rest of the family. My official diagnosis was "cyclothymic disorder," which basically means "mood swings." What sixteen-year-old girl doesn't have mood swings? This was before the Vietnam war, before the diagnosis of post-traumatic stress disorder (PTSD) was coined, which I think was a more accurate diagnosis for me at the time because of the psychological impact of my long-term exposure to incest. Post-traumatic stress disorder (PTSD) is a mental health condition that is triggered by a terrifying event. Symptoms may include flashbacks, nightmares, and severe anxiety, as well as uncontrollable thoughts about the event.

When I went back to review my records years later, my shrink, Dr. Bonner, told me that he would have diagnosed me with PTSD if it had been around at the time. Because neither my parents nor Dr. Bonner knew about the incest, they had no clue why I was acting out and doing bizarre things to seek attention. It was years after my discharge from the mental institution, shortly before my daughter was born, when I finally told my parents about the incest.

I couldn't talk about the incest to my psychiatrist because I didn't have the vocabulary to describe it, and I was too scared and ashamed. It was then that my psychiatrist decided to give me the drug, sodium pentathol, "the truth serum," which blocked my inhibitions and made it easier for me to freely discuss details of the incest. For years psychiatrists have used sodium pentathol to desensitize patients with deeply rooted fears and to help them recall painful, repressed memories. A Dutch professor, Jan Bastiaans, used the drug to help relieve trauma in survivors of the Holocaust. I've read that the drug doesn't always work for everyone, in terms of getting the truth out of them, but it worked for me. One thing for sure is that it makes you talk—a lot!

From the time I started having my period until the time that I finally told Dr. Bonner about the incest, I would panic every time my period was late. I would think that I was pregnant, even long after the abuse had stopped. Because I knew nothing about my own body, I was afraid a sperm got trapped inside me and had now created a baby. To give you an idea of how ignorant I was about the female body, I didn't know girls peed from a different place than the place we had sex. It wasn't until

Expect a Miracle

I was twenty years old and had an educational pelvic exam with my sex therapist, Sherry La Pointe, that things began to fall into place for me. My mother never had the birds and bees talk with me until after my engagement to my first husband. I was thirty years old! A little late, wasn't it? I imagine I knew more at age thirty than my mother knew her whole life. I don't think I was the only Southern girl who had this experience.

When I was pregnant with my daughter, my husband and I started having serious problems. My husband and I went to a marriage counselor, who recommended that I share the truth about the incest with my parents. He went on to explain that the secret was standing between me and my husband and that I would never know intimacy until I put the secret back into the family system where it belonged. But he also cautioned that the disclosure would be like throwing a boulder in the water: there would be many ripples, none of which I could anticipate or control.

My mother actually guessed what I was going to tell her before I told her. She was upset. Pissed off, my father advised the hospital where the perpetrator was going for treatment about the incest and the perpetrator admitted it. More mature and maybe a little relieved the secret was out, he apologized to me, saying that he knew that he was the reason I got so fat, heavily medicated, and locked up for such a long time. Little did he know the impact the incest had on my relationship with men—I couldn't have a normal relationship! As an adolescent, I would have sex with anybody that asked. I would have girlfriends, boyfriends, whatever. I learned to get love through sex. I didn't know the difference between sex and love; I thought sex was love. I thought abuse was love and I thought abusive painful sex was something to be expected and endured.

Fat, my face covered with acne, I was plagued with shame and starved for love. My self-esteem was at the lowest level imaginable. I looked for love in all the wrong places until I got venereal disease of the eye. Strangely enough, nearly all diseases which are considered to be sexually transmitted can affect the eye, especially diseases such as gonorrhea and chlamydia. In my case, only my eyes were infected.

Frustrated with life, I condemned myself regularly. I used to tell myself that I'm weak, fat, and ugly; that my face is covered with acne, that I have mousy brown hair, squinty eyes, stained teeth, and a pug nose; that I am an unattractive whore; that men only want me for sex or money; that I am an alcoholic, addict, stupid, and chronically mentally ill; that I can only learn to iron, can never go to college; that I am queer, always a bridesmaid, never a bride, unmarriageable, too hard to love, too much for everybody . . .

It's amazing that I lived to write about all this. I have since forgiven the perpetrator for the incest. I have no hard feelings toward him now. He didn't know any better. Also, when I look back on that segment of my life, I often get this unusual feeling that I signed up for all that before I was born. I don't think I was a victim at all. I think that we come into this life with our game plan for what we need to learn, and the perpetrator was just playing his role within that game plan. It has taken me many years to get this perspective. As a young adult, I didn't think like that. The way I look at it now, I needed those experiences to become the person I am today. Without the incest I would not have gotten a master's degree and become a therapist. I can't even begin to tell you the number of people I've been able to help as a result of my direct experience with incest. After years of counseling sex offenders, it has become clear to me that the victimizer had in some way been victimized himself.

Four

Addictions

> "Better a cruel truth than a comfortable delusion."
> — Edward Abbey

When my son was about a year old, I discovered why my mother was controlling my food so much. On my visit to the hospital for a routine checkup, I had an opportunity to read my records. It was disappointing to discover that every letter that my mother wrote to my doctor was about my appearance—acne, weight, stringy hair, clothing, and food. "We think if Marianne had her stomach stapled and just lost the weight she'd be fine," "Marianne's hair is oily," and on and on. There was nothing in any of the letters about Marianne's soul—her inner needs—the longings of her heart.

Before I started frequenting the hospital in response to weight problems, I was a regular customer at Lane Bryant and other stores for full-figured women. The only option for me as a child was Sears' chubby girls' department! Obviously, that was not what my mother envisioned for her only daughter. As I said earlier, when my parents stopped me from sucking my thumb at age eleven, I started smoking cigarettes. By age sixteen, I was totally addicted to smoking. I weighed 230 pounds, was heavily medicated, and could hardly do anything. I would just lie around, mope around, and wait, as if I was at the station waiting for a bus to arrive. I had no ambition or any need or desire to dream of a life beyond my current deplorable condition.

I began learning how to self-medicate. Since I was fourteen, I had been heavily medicated. It had been a long time since I knew what my body felt like without medication. If I was sad, the doctors gave me an upper; if I was happy, they gave me a tranquilizer. So I continued the routine even when I got off a particular medication. I would self-medicate, combining it with alcohol for greater effect. I think many people self-medicate to cope with this insane world. It starts with the sugary snacks in kindergarten. That's how it started for me. I usually justified my deeds by saying to myself, "I've always been a mental patient or a crazy, so why not be an alcoholic, too?"

"Alcoholic Anonymous (AA) accepts anybody," I'd say to myself, so I attended AA meetings, got sober, and eventually got addicted to meetings, which to me meant more social control. I've had experiences with different types of cults, including schools. And as far as I am concerned, AA is a spiritual cult. Many people say that without AA, they would never have let go of drinking, that it saved their lives. Actually, I think that most healthy people leave once they've been sober for a period of time. Many of the old-timers are really sick, disturbed individuals who enjoy having power over the newcomers and helping run their lives. People don't know why it works, and they don't know what works, but they just know they are different. Who knows why they are different. Let's face it, after repeating over and over to yourself, "I am powerless," "I am an alcoholic," "I am this," "I am that," it becomes a self-fulfilling prophecy. If you didn't believe these affirmations to begin with, you will after you've repeated these affirmations over and over again. Yes, I'm a pariah for leaving the cult, believe me. I am told by friends in AA that I am still gossiped about for leaving.

I came to think of AA as a cult for a number of reasons: mind control, group speak, and isolation from anyone not in the program. They tell you that you are powerless. They make you say over and over again, "I am an alcoholic," "I am powerless." They encourage you to give up your power to somebody else, a sponsor. If you try to challenge any of the old-timers, then you are in denial. I was in AA off and on from age sixteen until age fifty-two. I deprogrammed myself and helped deprogram a lot of people from it. They say they are the only path to recovery, despite the statistics. And the statistics are not true.

AA was supported by John Rockefeller, a member of the global elite. I wonder if that's why all the courts order people with drinking problems to attend 12-step programs, another way of keeping people down and slaves to the system. AA is an offshoot of a group called the Oxford Group, a tight little religious cult. They keep you vulnerable and in "group think." They keep you powerless, they keep you uncertain, they teach you that to drink is to die, they keep you afraid, they control your time, and they sponsor. Sponsoring means that somebody is your boss. You are not encouraged to think for yourself. There's reward and punishment. They will shun you if you don't do what is agreed upon. They beat themselves up at meetings with self-put-downs, self-flagellations, and they sort of clone each other and make up statistics. They are full of lies and deceit, and the meetings are full of sociopaths and people who are dependent on others. They excuse the most inexcusable behavior because they're alcoholics, after all. "It's ok because he or she has only been sober for thirty days." There are some meeting groups that are exceptions, but for the most part, this deceit I am describing is a reflection of my experience with AA. AA may have its place in helping get people clean and sober, but in my opinion it is not enough. There are other groups like SMART Recovery, Rational Recovery, and Women in Sobriety that have their place as well as therapy groups. AA did teach me to live in the moment, pray and meditate, and some useful tools for getting along with others and cleaning up my past.

Going to graduate school

I graduated from college and moved back to Arkansas to work for my dad at his John Deere dealership selling tractor parts. He treated his children worse than he treated other employees. I was the only family member at that particular dealership. Several employees were stealing from us but Daddy didn't seem to care. It bothered me because stealing was wrong and it bothered me that my father turned a blind eye to it. Although I was successful at my job, I was fed up. I told my dad that I couldn't work there anymore. It wasn't just the stealing. Being my father's employee meant that I always had to seek his approval constantly. It was like going to a dry well looking for water.

At that point in my life, I had three lives going on simultaneously. I'd get up and put on my brown pants and light brown shirt with the John Deere patch on one side and my name embroidered on the other side and head to work selling tractor parts. At the end of the day I would put on my silk dress and go be the daughter my mother wanted and head to the Junior League meetings to be involved in charity. From there I would put on jeans and a sweat shirt and head down to shoot pool and drink beer at the lesbian bar. Each life was separate and I lived in horror of friends in one life discovering the other two lives I led. The shame of each life darkened my world.

I left my job at my dad's company and went to work as a salesperson for a wholesale window treatment supplier. I had started dating Debbie, a social worker, at this time. She encouraged me to consider going to graduate school of social work. I told her there was no way I could do that. "I can't pass the admissions tests. I barely got into college with my SATs. I bet you I can't pass the GRE or MAT," I told her. She said, "You have to at least go audit one of Bob Sarver's classes." Bob was a larger than life social worker and lawyer who taught very interesting courses at the local university. I audited his class and loved him. He was most inspiring. After auditing three of his classes, he said to me, "Marianne, why don't you go to graduate school?" "I can't, Bob," I said. "I can't take those entrance exams. I will never pass them." He said, "Well, why don't you just apply?" I applied and they accepted me! Remarkably, I didn't have to take the entrance exams. I have no idea how that happened, and didn't ask.

Expect a Miracle

Although I lacked confidence in taking the graduate school entrance exams, I pulled off a grade point average (GPA) of a 4.0 in my first year at the University of Arkansas in Little Rock, and maintained that GPA until my graduation from graduate school. As my academic life progressed, my personal life began to change. I broke up with my girlfriend, Debbie. Not long after that, I met the man who would become my first husband. It was love at first sight. What I didn't know was that our relationship would rank as the greatest drama of my life.

Five

Dealing with the Influence of My Heritage

"Condemnation without investigation is the height of ignorance."
— Albert Eienstein

I met my first husband, Dale, at Alcoholics Anonymous (AA). We were at a party playing Trivial Pursuit and he was on my team. He was full of trivia, handsome, and charming, with his beautiful blue eyes, dark hair, and a goatee. But depending on the moment, he either looked like a movie star or the devil. He had a huge, colorful tattoo on his right arm and reminded me of a classical felon. Interestingly enough, it turned out he was a felon. I think he got his tattoo in prison.

Unbeknownst to me, he hadn't been sober for long and there were other issues I would later discover. He was a social worker

Expect a Miracle

and had been ordered to either go to rehab or lose his job. But once he left for rehab, he got fired anyway. The year was 1985. I had been out of college three years and just started graduate school in social work at University of Arkansas at Little Rock. I was also dealing with a massive weight loss of 150 pounds, which left excess skin hanging down from every part of my body. I had also just broken up with my girlfriend of two years, and my self-esteem was miserably low. I was ashamed for having been in a relationship with a woman and for having been institutionalized for many years. In addition, I felt like a stranger in my new thinner body. So you can imagine how flattered I must have felt to have this handsome, smart, and charming man take interest in me.

I checked into the hospital to have plastic surgery, to hide, and to remove all of the ugly excess skin. When I was in my room recovering from surgery, with ace bandages on my arms, chest, and stomach, I got an intimidating surprise. Dale came to visit me! He brought a teddy bear and balloon. I was horrified and exhilarated at the same time: horrified that he saw me in my condition, yet exhilarated that he cared enough to come with caring gifts! That did it. I fell head over heels in love.

He asked me to marry him and I had no idea I could say no. After all, if he wanted me I must be worth something, right? He went and asked for my father's blessings, and the engagement was in progress, despite warnings from my AA friends. They strongly advised me against marrying Dale, saying that I didn't know the real Dale and his history. But I was convinced that he just hadn't received the love he needed in order to be all he could be, and I knew I could provide that for him. I have a history of seeing the pretty golden light inside a tornado and ignoring the dark destructive wind on the outside. I always got involved with the potential, not the reality. Dale had been married twice but I was not alarmed that I was wife number three because he assured me that his first wife was a narcissist and that his second wife was crazy. I was happy that he didn't have or want any children because I didn't either. I was thirty years old and my biological clock had yet to start ticking.

Being the only girl in the South, my mother and I began to plan the big wedding, and a big one it was! For our wedding present, my parents offered us a choice of a lump sum of money or a honeymoon in Europe. Dale wanted the money, so I agreed. I really wanted the trip to Europe. I still haven't been to Europe. We went to Hot Springs for the weekend to attend the Alcoholic Anonymous Convention as part of our honeymoon. We did go parasailing to take a break from the convention. My parents were well loved in the community and we were showered with parties and presents. The wedding and reception were a lot of fun. The problems began the next morning when my new husband got up and wanted to go have breakfast with one of his guy friends—a guy whom I later learned was his drug friend buddy. Furthermore, I came to realize that although Dale wasn't drinking at the time, he was addicted to prescription pain pills. This taught me to pay attention to warnings from those with more objective eyes.

Dale wanted to move to Denver and get his PhD, so I agreed. I sold my duplex, gave away my dogs (the apartment we could afford didn't allow pets, a trade I later regretted), transferred to the University of Denver, and began my second year of graduate school. I had a 4.0 average leaving the University of Arkansas at Little Rock. So I was in competition with myself to maintain that GPA while getting my PhT (Putting hubby through) at the same time.

Dale got his PhD in social work in record time, two years! He often complained of cluster migraines and back pain and had to go to doctors and to the Emergency Room to get relief. I felt very sorry for him as he was working so hard to get his PhD. I knew the stress was killing him.

As luck would have it, I got pregnant. Must have been meant to be, because as sexually promiscuous as I had been, never using birth control, I had never gotten pregnant before. When I was about six weeks pregnant, Dale received a manuscript in the mail and it was his first wife's autobiography. She wanted Dale to read it and approve it. He wanted me to read it, too. After all, we were expecting a child and planning a family, and our children might one day read this stuff. Read it, I did. I was horrified! He was, too! He got her to delete a lot of the bad things about him and his family, but the damage had already been done as far as I was concerned. I couldn't believe the sick stuff I read.

When I was three months pregnant I went for my checkup and my doctor told me the baby was dead and that I would have to have a D and C. I was in shock again. I had already redefined myself as a mother and was anxiously expecting the baby. Now all that had suddenly changed. I was no longer a mother. Dale seemed rather unmoved by the event. He continued to focus on his school work as if nothing happened. Not me; I was an emotional wreck and was eagerly looking for a way to let go of my deep feelings of loss.

I had always wanted to snow ski ever since we moved to Denver but couldn't because of my pregnancy. When I got out of the hospital, I decided to go for it. Take it from me, that is not the thing to do when you are grief-stricken and your life feels so out of control anyway. I was miserable. When we told Dale's mother that we had lost the baby, she said, "So what, it was just a seed anyway." People can be so insensitive at times like this. I learned a lot from my doctor about the effects of miscarriage on expecting mothers. He told me I wouldn't heal until I had a live baby in my hands, and he was right.

Everywhere I went I saw women with children; I hated them for having what I had lost. Soon I was back to therapy for support in my grieving process. My doctor said that my husband and I should wait six months before trying for another baby. That was the longest six months of my life, and when we did try again I immediately got pregnant with my son, Clay. He was born after thirty-one hours of labor. It was a snowy day, and my parents were present. Dale was there for the delivery and put on quite a show for my parents and me. He was absolutely proud and happy! Clay was born just a few weeks before Dale was awarded his PhD. I had been out of school for a year and was working in the Victim Assistance Program in Englewood, Colorado.

Expect a Miracle

After Dale graduated he wanted to move back to Arkansas. I didn't want to because I was happy in Denver. My career was going well. Nevertheless, I agreed to move to Arkansas with him. I had long been trained as a Southern girl to give up my life for the man. He really wanted to go to Fayetteville and get on the faculty of Arkansas where his father was working, but that had to wait. There were no positions open.

We both went to work starting up a Charter Hospital and that's when I was on the Today Show. Charter was a corporate group of mental hospitals and we were on the startup team of a brand new hospital in Little Rock. Not long after I started work there, a cluster suicide occurred in a high school in a small town about thirty-five miles away. Five boys went into the classroom and blew their brains out in front of their classmates. Immediately I was dispatched to lead a team into the schools to help students, teachers, and families cope with the situation. Some of the officials did not want us there because our presence attracted more media attention. It was a major news event and the suicide was speculated to have involved satanic worship. Since I led a crisis intervention team into the schools, I was asked to appear on NBC's Today Show for an interview.

That was my moment of fame and I was so excited! Look how far I had come! From chronically mentally ill to a therapist on national television! I called my parents to share the news and they said they would watch it. NBC sent a chauffeured limo stocked with booze and ice to come get me and took me down to the green room at the NBC affiliate in Little Rock. When the interview started, they also had an expert from Boston. My marketing director had instructed me to take charge of that interview: "I don't care how you do it, just take charge and it will be successful." Of course his concern was the publicity Charter would get. I agreed, although I had never been on TV before and wasn't quite sure how I would pull it off.

When Deborah Norville started the interview, I realized her approach was to use the expert from Boston to show the Southern girl how it is done. The interviewer asked me a few questions and then she went to the lady from Boston. I asked the expert where she trained. She had trained in the same school in Denver where I received my training. I said, "How many cluster suicides have you worked?" "None," she said. I was working my second one. With that, she was taken off the screen and I was interviewed exclusively. I had an asymmetrical haircut at the time. I usually wear my hair in nontraditional styles that my father called my "go to hell" hairdos! After my appearance on TV my mother called to report that she had watched me on TV as had my Aunt Mary Jane, and Mary Jane wanted to know if that was how I was wearing my hair now? My bubble was burst. I had thought my parents would finally be proud of me, I had become somebody, and that's all they had to say?

I got too big for my britches and my ego began to destroy me. My self-esteem was so low at the time, I was with a verbally and emotionally abusive man at the time, and I couldn't handle the success. I think Dale was threatened by my success but he had security that I would stay because we had Clay. He knew I valued family and I would not want to raise a child alone. He also knew that I had a high tolerance for insanity. We had lots of problems, but at that time they were mostly typical newlywed adjustments, or so I thought. We hired a lawyer to get Dale's criminal records expunged successfully so that we could proceed with a normal white-collar life.

Dale applied for a job in the social work program at the U of A at Fayetteville and was hired, so we moved there. We decided I would open a private practice so my schedule would be flexible and I wouldn't have to put Clay in day care. I didn't feel adequate or competent for private practice. I had been in therapy most of my life, and I still felt "crazy" much of the time. Dale encouraged me and said he would help. I talked to my former therapist and mentor, Mary Roush, about it, and she encouraged me too, saying that I would get the confidence and the remainder of my healing from the job. She asked me how I was taking care of my boundaries. I didn't even know what the word meant: not a good thing for a new therapist opening up a private practice. But she reassured me, "Opening a practice is like becoming a mother. If you wait until you feel prepared you will never do it. You just go and do it, and the rest will follow." I was told it would take five years to build a practice, but my schedule was full in six months. Again more success than I was ready for. I had to hire other therapists to help out. Dale also helped me in the practice but his focus was on teaching at the U of A, doing research, and publishing—wanting to match the esteem held for his dad, a doctorate in science. Like my father, when Dale had a job, he was a workaholic. He would throw himself into his work 2,000 percent.

My second child, Molly, was born three weeks after Clay turned two. Dale began disappearing for days at a time. My parents came to take care of Clay while I was in the hospital taking care of Molly, but I didn't end up staying overnight. Molly's birth was easy, and the hospital nurses were busy taking care of millionaire J. B. Hunt's twin granddaughters so they weren't very responsive to me. Molly was born just after one in the afternoon and we were home in time for supper. Thank God my parents were there to help me because Dale was acting very strange and not involved at all. He almost dropped Molly twice and I was scared of him and for the children.

One night I woke up and Dale was gone. The car was in the garage, his keys were there, but he and his wallet were gone. I had two babies so I couldn't go look for him. I was terrified. All of my abandonment issues came up. Was he leaving us? Where was he? I called his mother and stepfather, who asked if I had checked the Emergency Room (ER). I said, "No, why?" He said that Dale had a habit of faking kidney stones and going to the ER for morphine. I was shocked and angry. Why had no one told me this before? Just then, Dale walked in with our neighbor, a urologist, and was loaded up on morphine. The doctor explained to me that Dale had come knocking on his door complaining of kidney stones and that he had taken him to the hospital and treated him. I was too tired to fight, I had a full load of clients the next day, and he was too doped up to talk, so we both went to sleep.

This pattern continued for some time. It progressed to a point where Dale would drive up and down the interstate highway, across several states, hitting up ERs and pharmacies for morphine, paregoric, and codeine. He would wear his suit and tie, carry his briefcase, prick his finger and put blood in his urine, get the morphine, get discharged, put makeup on the IV bruise on his arm, and head to the next ER. Occasionally I would get a call from him after he had been gone several days, asking me to pick him up because the ER wouldn't let him drive. By then I was strong enough to say no. As time went on, the Emergency Rooms got suspicious and started communicating with each other, eventually cutting him off—in other words, they refused to admit him any longer.

From there on, Dale went back to pain pills and street drugs. He became very dangerous, carried a gun, began drinking alcohol as well, and was verbally, emotionally, and sexually abusive to me. Every time he drank, he got mean. He encouraged me to drink as well, assuring me I never was an alcoholic anyway, and that even if I had been, with all the neurofeedback I had done I must be cured. I liked the idea and one night when we went to a comedy club, at his suggestion, I drank. Alcohol was not a problem for me then and wasn't for several months.

As early as age two, my daughter could predict when her father was going to go off on "high lonesome," as my friend Sam called it. We ended up having to go on the run from him. We stayed in a battered women's shelter and had to put him in treatment several times. The last time I sent him for treatment, he called me from the hospital. I thought he was calling to apologize for all his troubles and promise to do better. Instead he told me I needed to have an AIDS test, because he had been using needles. I couldn't believe it! How much more can I take? I arranged and took the test.

Dr. Whitney, who conducted the test, consulted in my private practice: if my patients needed medical care, I referred them to him. One Friday afternoon, I came out of my office after my last patient and Dr. Whitney was sitting in my waiting room with concern written all over his face. He said, "Marianne, I've got something I need to talk to you about." "Oh no, not again," I said. I thought it was about my husband. He said, "No, it's about your AIDS test. You've got AIDS." "What?" I screamed. "You've got AIDS," he repeated. "You sure?" I questioned. "Yeah," he responded. They had just come out with the PCR Assay, a DNA test, and there are no false positives. "You've got it. It's a DNA test. You need to get your affairs in order," he said with confidence. For some odd reason, MDs seem to enjoy delivering bad news with certainty. I flipped out and totally lost it. I called my parents to tell them. My babies were one and three. Who's going to raise my kids? Dale wouldn't because he's in rehab. I just went nuts thinking, I'm dying of AIDS. I started drinking and drugging to cope and ended up drunk in the ditch with a DUI.

I frantically started looking around for a solution. I heard that San Diego was the best place to do AIDS treatment. As far as I was concerned, AIDS was a death sentence. I had a friend, a nurse who did in-home health care with AIDS patients, who suggested I take the ELISA and Western blot—older, more established tests at the time—just to see what the results would be. I asked the doctor who had given me the original diagnosis about these tests, and he said, "Oh no, you don't need to take that." I said, "What the hell am I gonna do, then?" I went ahead and took the tests, and the results came back negative. What a relief! I discovered that there ARE false positives, mostly due to human error. I tested every six months for the next three years to be sure it was true. It was a crazy experience! It took me years to get over it. Dale told me at the time that he prayed that I didn't have AIDS and told God he would devote his life to AIDS victims if I would just be spared. As far as I know he never fulfilled his end of the bargain.

As I came close to what I considered to be an emotional, spiritual, physical (financial) bankruptcy, I filed for divorce with Dale. It was easily granted, along with the best visitation package I could ask for: supervised, unless Dale demonstrated three months of continuous sobriety. We divorced but didn't separate until much later. I was addicted to him as well as the idea of a family and wouldn't let go. I even went so far as getting a marriage license to remarry him and going on a cruise with him. I should have known better. He and I had gone on a cruise with the kids, together with my parents, on the Big Red Boat. He got off the boat and made horrible scary drug deals in every country we docked in and barely made it back on the boat before it left. You know the definition of insanity? Doing the same thing over and over again and expecting different results? I was insane. The best predictor of future behavior is often found in past behavior, but I so wanted a family and everything to be okay, so I tried again. The same things happened on that cruise except this time I left the kids with a nanny.

I was even stupid enough to try crack cocaine with him one time. Dale was heavy into it and suggested I try it, too. He thought I would like it. When I was a teenager, the "fat" doctor put me on speed to lose weight. In high school, my shrink in Little Rock did the same thing to help me concentrate, and I had done cocaine and ecstasy (back then it was called MDMA) in college and liked it. I did not become addicted, but I had heard that with crack you are addicted from your first use. I was scared, but I tried it. Fortunately I hated it. I felt like I was being shot with 1000 volts of electricity, skin crawling, sweating, and tremendous anxiety. One puff and I said no more. Just like the alcohol, he was trying to get me to do all the stuff he did, to make me look as bad as he did, to use as a form of control, like blackmail.

It was Halloween, months after our divorce. Dale and I took the kids to the carnival at their school. I was dressed as a bag lady. After the carnival I agreed to help the other mothers clean up while Dale took the kids to his apartment to spend the night. After we finished cleaning up, we went out for drinks. In the meantime, Dale was calling my house repeatedly and leaving messages. There were no cells phones back then. He became increasingly upset with each subsequent message. When I got home and heard the messages, I called him. He was furious that I had gone out and demanded I come get the kids or he would leave them out on his balcony.

I was terrified. It was about one o'clock in the morning. I told him that I couldn't right away because I had been drinking. I told him that if I had a chance to eat and drink some Tab, I would be right over. He kept calling and eventually I went over there. Upon getting to his apartment, he woke the kids up and told them that their mother was drunk and had come to kidnap them. Now remember, we were therapists working together with adult children of alcoholics. I knew the psychological scarring this would cause for the kids and so did he. I was horrified and began planning my escape. It was the middle of the night in a horrible apartment complex in a dangerous neighborhood. He grabbed my car keys and locked his apartment door. Standing against the door, he said that I was drunk, and he refused to let me leave. I picked up my daughter, Molly, with her pull-ups, blanket, and pacifier, and held her. Clay went back to bed to sleep. I begged Dale to let us leave. Molly was crying and so was I. He pushed both of us outside and locked the door behind us, saying he was going to call the police.

I stood in the parking lot with the baby in my arms, waiting on the police. A car drove up, and fortunately they were a nice couple. They offered help. I followed them to their house and was able to call the police from there. They indicated that Dale had called and that they were on their way. I was instructed to stand outside and wait. I could tell by the dispatcher's response that she thought I was the bad guy. It was freezing outside but I had to wait out there.

When the cops got there, one went in to talk with Dale and Clay while the other invited Molly and me into his warm car. He was a young guy and a nice officer. He began to confide in me, saying that if I told anybody what he was about to tell me, that he would swear I was a liar. He didn't want to get in trouble with the other cops or his department. He proceeded to give me one piece of advice that was on the edge of being legal. He confided in me that he was sometimes psychic and that he had had a vision earlier in the day about Dale. He said that Dale was the kind of guy that if he couldn't have his wife, nobody else could. He described Dale physically without ever meeting him and was accurate. He said Dale wanted a police report to later use in court against me. He said that when Dale called the police he told them he had custody and I was over there drunk trying to take the kids away.

Because I didn't take along my court documents to Dale's apartment that early morning, I couldn't prove anything. The officer explained that if I were to leave the kids with Dale, no report would be made, but if I wanted to leave, since I had admitted I had been drinking, they would have to do a breathalyzer, and regardless of results, a report would be made. The officer indicated that it was already three o'clock in the morning, and Dale will be taking the kids to school at 7:30 a.m. So, I could pick them up then, from school. He advised me to get the hell out of Dodge and lose my identity.

Leaving the kids that night with Dale was one of the hardest things I have ever done, but I did it. Thankfully he had them in school the next day and I went and picked them up. In view of his irregular behavior, I had to enforce a supervised visitation. Furious, he sued me for contempt of court and sought joint custody and reimbursement of his attorney's fees. It cost me

Expect a Miracle

$5,000 to fight him but I won quite easily, for he showed up in court for the case high on crack.

Around Christmas that year, Dale had a massive coronary attack and was fighting for his life in the hospital. The kids were called in twice in five days to say their goodbyes to their dying father. Not surprising, on the fifth day, Dale broke out of the hospital, with all the attached monitors going off as he flew out of the front door wearing his hospital gown with his butt showing, headed down the street to a convenience store to get cigarettes. That's Dale for you. As an aside, for some odd reason, insane people have an unusually high ability to survive.

When I finally did separate from Dale on every level, he resorted to psychological terrorism. You're probably wondering what I mean by psychological terrorism. Dale began to stalk me. Everywhere I went, I'd look up and he was there. Scared, I got a burglar alarm installed and convinced a big Mexican friend of mine to stay at our house, armed with a gun.

One morning, as I opened up the garage to go to work, Dale was standing outside of it. I had a restraining order on him but he always escaped before the police got there. One night I heard somebody outside under the front deck beating on it. Another time somebody slipped inside the fence of my back yard, in spite of six inches of snow on the ground, turned on my garden hose and left it running in the middle of the night. I had no proof but I could only assume it was Dale. I didn't know anybody else who would do something like that. His previous therapist had diagnosed him as a sociopath in front of large audience during a family reconstruction weekend. His signs were undeniably diagnostic of a sociopath.

One of the features of sociopaths is lack of remorse or guilt. When Molly was about two years old, I found a feral cat and its kittens in our yard. I'm an animal lover. My friends call me Ellie May. I can't stand to see animals suffer. One of the kittens was suffering. I told Dale I was going to take the suffering kitten to the veterinarian after I finished giving my daughter a bath. "That wouldn't be necessary, the kitten should just be killed now," he said. We started fighting over it, and I thought we had an understanding. I went ahead and started to give Molly a bath in her little tub which I placed inside the kitchen sink. Suddenly I heard a banging noise outside. When I looked out the window, I was horrified. Dale had covered the suffering kitten with a trash bag and was pounding it to death with a shovel. I screamed at the top of my lungs, scaring my little toddler. That could be Clay, Molly, or me, instead of a kitten. I got the message. After killing the kitten, he carried on like nothing happened. Sociopaths' lack of remorse or guilt is associated with their remarkable ability to rationalize their behavior and to shrug off personal responsibility for actions that cause shock and disappointment to family, friends, associates, and others who have played by the rules. They usually have handy excuses for their behavior, and in some cases they deny that it happened at all.

In an attempt to understand the disease, I began to work with Reid Meloy, an expert on sociopathy, and read all his books. In this book I use both the terms sociopath and psychopath to refer to the same set of behaviors. Successful treatment of sociopaths is based on many factors, one of them being their degree of intellect. Dale was way too smart to respond to treatment. I learned that sociopaths lead with pity and take advantage of the good parts of you. I learned that the people who fall victim to sociopaths are people who refuse to believe there are people like that. It was explained to me by my therapist that he was an emotional predator. He got his sense of self from me. The one thing psychopaths can't tolerate is rejection. In order for me to survive, I had to remain emotionless around him and give him no clue of how I felt because he read and manipulated me off of those clues. I had felt sorry for him as an addict and it was explained to me that he was not. He used whatever substance was necessary to create the sense of self he needed to pull off his next con.

I moved to California and started a new life. Dale followed for a little while but decided to go to work in a treatment program where he met a patient, his next wife/victim, Erica. The kids and I were happy he was marrying Erica, not a person with a name that started with an M. His mother and his first three wives all had names that started with M. Dale called me on a Wednesday and said he and Erica were getting married on Thursday, the next day. They wanted Molly to be the flower girl and Clay the ring bearer. "Would you get them clothes and have them there tomorrow?" he persuaded me. Dale had supervised visitation only at that time so I would have to take them if they were to go. I tried to help the kids have a relationship with their dad as best as I could, so I agreed. Incidentally, I had been advised by my therapist that he would not leave me alone until he remarried. I was happy he was getting married. He and his wife asked me to sign for them as a witness because their signer was late.

Although I thought all I had to do was sign the paper, the justice of the peace insisted that I stand at the back of the courtroom as witness. I was horrified but ended up being glad I did because as she said, "Do you, Dale, take thee, Erica Marianne…?" both of our kids busted out laughing. We all realized he had not broken the "M" pattern after all.

Dale and Erica moved to Texas and Dale went to work in a social work program in a university there. They started having problems immediately and she began calling me for help. He had become physically violent with her. On Christmas Eve, the kids got a collect call from their father, calling from jail, one of many occasions to come. He was there on charges of attempted felony murder of a police officer. That began a series of arrests that ended up putting him in prison for two more years. When I met my current husband, Bill, Dale had just gotten out of prison and moved closer to our kids and me in the same little town. Today he is working in a treatment center where he once was getting help. I, on the other hand, moved to Hawaii with my husband, Bill, for a more peaceful life.

Six

Symptoms of Sociopaths You Might Overlook

"To seek the truth, for the sake of knowing the truth, is one of the noblest objects a man can live for."

—Dean Inge

I have decided to include a chapter on sociopaths in my book because I know this information can be useful to many readers. If I had known more about this disease, its signs and symptoms, I would have left my husband long ago, before he was able to do so much damage to me and my kids. Martha Hudson, in her book, Sociopath Next Door, estimates that as many as one out of ten people are sociopaths, so there may well be one in your life!

Other than my own experience with my ex-husband, Dale, much of the information in this chapter is excerpted from a previously published article by one of the leading experts in the research of psychopaths, Dr. Robert Hare. His credentials are extensive.

To provide a quick summary, he is an emeritus professor of psychology at the University of British Columbia, where he has taught and conducted research for more than four decades, and president of Darkstone Research Group Ltd., a forensic research and consulting firm. He has devoted most of his academic career to the investigation of psychopathy, its nature, assessment, and implications for mental health and criminal justice. He is the author of several books, including Without Conscience: The Disturbing World of the Psychopaths Among Us, and more than one hundred scientific articles on psychopathy.

To start, psychopaths are glib and superficial. Like Dale, who swept me off my feet when I first met him, psychopaths are often witty and articulate. They can be amusing and entertaining conversationalists, ready with a quick and clever comeback, and can tell unlikely but convincing stories that cast themselves in a good light. They can be very effective in presenting themselves well and are often very likable and charming.

They are also egocentric and grandiose. Psychopaths have a narcissistic and grossly inflated view of their self-worth and importance, a truly astounding egocentricity and sense of entitlement. They see themselves as the center of the universe, as superior beings who are justified in living according to their own rules. What drove my husband to get a PhD and to seek a teaching and research position in the same university where his father taught was to outdo his father. He was so determined with his studies that when I had a miscarriage with our first child, it didn't seem to bother him a bit. He continued with his studies as if nothing happened and hardly talked much about it thereafter.

Psychopaths are seldom embarrassed about their legal, financial, or personal problems. Rather, they see them as temporary setbacks, the results of bad luck, unfaithful friends, or an unfair and incompetent system. Dale lived in one of the worst neighborhoods in town and it didn't bother him a bit. He would rather spend his money on pharmaceutical drugs and crack cocaine than take better care of himself and his family.

There's this lack of remorse or guilt that is a part of the makeup of psychopaths. They show a stunning lack of concern for the devastating effects their actions have on others. Often they are completely forthright about the matter, calmly stating that they have no sense of guilt, are not sorry for the pain and destruction they have caused, and that there is no reason for them to be concerned. When my ex called me in the middle of the night to come pick up the kids and later threw me out the door with my baby in the middle of winter, I don't think he was able to think that through. I don't think he wondered what effect his behavior would cause the kids in years to come.

Dr. Hare says that psychopaths' lack of remorse or guilt is associated with a remarkable ability to rationalize their behavior and to shrug off personal responsibility for actions that cause shock and disappointment to family, friends, associates and others who have played by the rules. Usually they have handy excuses for their behavior, and in some cases they deny that it happened at all. So denial is a big part of it.

Expect a Miracle

They lack empathy. The feelings of other people are of no concern to psychopaths. They view people as little more than objects to be used for their own gratification. The weak and the vulnerable—whom they mock, rather than pity—are favorite targets. They are indifferent to the rights and suffering of family members and strangers alike. If they do maintain ties with their spouses or children it is only because they see their family members as possessions, much like their stereos or automobiles.

Because of their inability to appreciate the feelings of others, some psychopaths are capable of behavior that normal people find not only horrific but baffling. For example, they can torture and mutilate their victims with about the same sense of concern that we feel when we carve a turkey for Thanksgiving dinner. However, except in movies and books, very few psychopaths commit crimes of this sort. Their callousness typically emerges in less dramatic, though still devastating, ways: parasitically bleeding other people of their possessions, savings, and dignity; aggressively doing and taking what they want; shamefully neglecting the physical and emotional welfare of their families; engaging in an unending series of casual, impersonal, and trivial sexual relationships; and so forth.

My ex was deceitful and manipulative, which is typical of psychopaths. When he called me to pick up the kids from his apartment, he called the police and turned the story around, telling them that I was there to kidnap them. He also manipulated me to come to his apartment at one o'clock in the morning even though I told him that I had been drinking. He wanted the police to meet a drunken mother. Lying, deceiving and manipulation are natural talents for psychopaths. Given their glibness and the facility with which they lie, it is not surprising that psychopaths successfully cheat, bilk, defraud, con, and manipulate people and have not the slightest compunction about doing so. They are often forthright in describing themselves as con men, hustlers, or fraud artists. Their statements often reveal their belief that the world is made up of "givers and takers," predators and prey, and that it would be very foolish not to exploit the weaknesses of others.

Some of their operations are elaborate and well thought out, whereas others are quite simple: stringing along several women at the same time, or convincing family members and friends that money is needed "to bail me out of a jam." Whatever the scheme, it is carried off in a cool, self-assured, brazen manner. Dale, a PhD psychotherapist, was in and out of jail: Go figure.

Psychopaths also have shallow emotions. According to Dr. Robert Hare, psychopaths seem to suffer a kind of emotional poverty that limits the range and depth of their feelings. While at times they appear cold and unemotional, they are prone to dramatic, shallow, and short-lived displays of feeling. Careful observers are left with the impression that they are play-acting and that little is going on below the surface. Hare indicated that laboratory experiments using biomedical recorders have shown that psychopaths lack the physiological responses normally associated with fear. The significance of this finding is that, for most people, the fear produced by threats of pain or punishment is an unpleasant emotion and a powerful motivator of behavior. Not so with psychopaths; they merrily plunge on, perhaps knowing what might happen but not really caring. My ex knew very well that emergency rooms had caught on to the fact that he was faking kidney stones. Do you think that stopped him from hitting more emergency rooms for drugs? No! Do you think he was concerned that they would report him? No! Do you think he was concerned that he would lose his professional license as a therapist? Hell, no! None of those things probably crossed his mind, which leads us to the next trait of psychopaths—impulsiveness.

Psychopaths are unlikely to spend much time weighing the pros and cons of a course of action or considering the possible consequences. "I did it because I felt like it," is a common response. According to Dr. Hare, more than displays of temper, impulsive acts often result from an aim that plays a central role in most of the psychopath's behavior: to achieve immediate satisfaction, pleasure, or relief. So family members, employers, and co-workers typically find themselves standing around asking themselves what happened—jobs are quit, relationships broken off, plans changed, houses ransacked, people hurt, often for what appears to be little more than a whim. Psychopaths tend to live day to day and change their plans frequently. They give little serious thought to the future and worry about it even less.

If you are dating a psychopath or married to one, by now you should be used to poor behavior. Research shows that in psychopaths, inhibitory controls are weak, and the slightest provocation is sufficient to overcome them. As a result, psychopaths are short tempered or hotheaded and tend to respond to frustration, failure, discipline, and criticism with sudden violence, threats, and verbal abuse. They take offense easily and become angry and aggressive over trivialities, often in a context that appears inappropriate to others. But their outbursts, extreme as they may be, are generally short-lived, and they quickly resume acting as if nothing out of the ordinary has happened. Although psychopaths have a "hair trigger" and readily initiate aggressive displays, their ensuing behavior is not out of control. On the contrary, when psychopaths "blow their stack" it is as if they are having a temper tantrum; they know exactly what they are doing. Their aggressive displays are "cold"; they lack the intense emotional arousal experienced by others when they lose their temper. It's not unusual for psychopaths to inflict serious physical or emotional damage on others, sometimes routinely, and yet refuse to acknowledge that they have a problem controlling their tempers. In most cases, they see their aggressive displays as natural responses to provocation.

My marriage with my ex was action packed. There was always a crisis to respond to, whether it was calling the police, taking him to the hospital, or bailing out of jail. The need for excitement is just a part of being a psychopath. They have an ongoing and excessive need for excitement—they long to live in the fast lane or on the edge, where the action is. In many cases the action involves breaking the rules. Some psychopaths use a wide variety of drugs as part of their general search for something new and exciting, and they often move from place to place and job to job searching for a fresh buzz. Many psychopaths describe "doing crime" for excitement or thrills. The flip side of this yearning for excitement is an inability to tolerate routine or monotony. Psychopaths are easily bored. You are not likely to find them engaged in occupations or activities that are dull, repetitive, or that require intense concentration over long periods.

Lack of responsibility is another characteristic of psychopaths. My husband's sense of responsibility to the kids is zero. He did help initially, but as he got overtaken by his tendencies, he was in no position to care for a family. Obligations and commitments mean nothing to psychopaths. Their good intentions—"I'll never cheat on you again"—are promises written on the wind. Truly horrendous credit histories, for example, reveal the lightly taken debt, the shrugged-off loan, the empty pledge to contribute to a child's support. The irresponsibility and unreliability of psychopaths extend to every part of their lives. Their performance on the job is erratic, with frequent absences, misuse of company resources, violations of company policy, and general untrustworthiness. They do not honor formal or implied commitments to people, organizations, or principles. Indifference to the welfare of children—their own as well as those of a man or woman they happen to be living with at the time—is a common theme among psychopaths. Psychopaths see children as an inconvenience. Typically, they leave children on their own for extended periods or in the care of unreliable sitters.

Psychopaths are frequently successful in talking their way out of trouble—"I've learned my lesson"; "You have my word that it won't happen again"; "It was simply a big misunderstanding"; "Trust me." They are almost as successful in convincing the criminal justice system of their good intentions and their trustworthiness. Although they frequently manage to obtain probation, a suspended sentence, or early release from prison, they simply ignore the conditions imposed by the courts. Often with these characters their words and actions are totally inconsistent, so when people's words and actions don't match, I have learned to pay attention to their actions.

Most psychopaths begin to exhibit serious behavioral problems at an early age. These might include persistent lying, cheating, theft, fire setting, truancy, class disruption, substance abuse, vandalism, violence, bullying, running away, and precocious sexuality. Because many children exhibit some of these behaviors at one time or another, especially children raised in violent neighborhoods or in disrupted or abusive families, it is important to emphasize that the psychopath's history of such behaviors is more extensive and serious than that of most others, even when compared with those of siblings and friends raised in similar settings.

Early cruelty to animals is usually a sign of serious emotional or behavioral problems. Cruelty to other children—including siblings—is often part of the young psychopath's inability to experience the sort of empathy that checks normal people's impulses to inflict pain, even when enraged.

Psychopaths are known for antisocial behavior. They consider the rules and expectations of society inconvenient and unreasonable impediments to their inclinations and wishes. They make their own rules, both as children and as adults. Many of the antisocial acts of psychopaths lead to criminal convictions. Even within prison populations psychopaths stand out, largely because their antisocial and illegal activities are more varied and frequent than are those of other criminals.

Not all psychopaths end up in jail. Many of the things they do escape detection or prosecution or are on the "shady side of the law." For them, antisocial behavior may consist of phony stock promotions, questionable business and professional practices, spousal or child abuse, and so forth. Many others do things that, although not illegal, are unethical, immoral, or harmful to others: philandering, cheating on a spouse, financial or emotional neglect of family members, irresponsible use of company resources or funds, to name but a few. The problem with behaviors of this sort is that they are difficult to document and evaluate without the active cooperation of family, friends, acquaintances, and business associates.

To summarize, psychopaths are not the only ones who lead socially deviant lifestyles. For example, many criminals have some of the characteristics described above, but because they are capable of feeling guilt, remorse, empathy, and strong emotions, they are not considered psychopaths. A diagnosis of psychopathy is made only when there is solid evidence that the individual matches the complete profile—that is, has most of the above symptoms.

If you expect sociopaths to have a crazy or sinister appearance, you're sadly mistaken. Sociopaths look nondescript, average, or attractive—just like anybody else. Sociopaths come from all walks of life—including well-educated, well-off families. Many sociopaths, therefore, have good social graces. They know how to dress and how to behave in polite society. This doesn't stop them from lying, cheating, and stealing. On the contrary, it makes their deceptions easier. Sociopaths from middle-class or privileged backgrounds often excel at white-collar crime—fraud, phony stock schemes, embezzlement.

There you have it. Again, I wish I had known all this when I met my first husband. I would have definitely made better choices. But it's all experience. I'm glad I survived it, together with the kids. Now, try not to jump to conclusions by calling your spouse or significant other a psychopath. They have to meet most of the traits described in the chapter to be considered as one, and they still need to be evaluated and diagnosed by a qualified mental health care professional. That said, be alert and steer clear from anyone who seems determined to seek your sympathy or ruin your life. Get help as quickly as possible if your partner begins to exhibit some of the tendencies described in this chapter.

Seven

From Revolving Closet Door to Real Love

"Cowardice asks the question: "Is it safe?"
Expediency asks the question: "Is it politic?"
Vanity asks the question: "Is it popular?"
But conscience asks: "Is it Right?"
And there comes a time when one must take a position that is neither safe, nor politic, nor popular but he must do it because conscience tells him it is right."

—Martin Luther King

I thought sex was love, because that was the only way I knew to get love. My father always told me that all people wanted me for was sex or money. I didn't know the difference between sex and love. I was afraid of men and I couldn't have sex unless I was drunk. In college I started hanging around gay guys. My best friend, Randy, was gay. I just adored him. He had the same birthday as my father. He died of AIDS in his thirties. A girl who hung around gay guys and was not gay was called a fag hag. I wanted to fit in by hanging around gay guys but, once again, I was on the outside looking in. Throughout my life, I was desperate to be a part of something. I have never felt like I fit until later in life when I moved to the island of Kauai, in Hawaii. It's the only place I have fit in, ever! That's why I decided to make it my home.

I didn't want to be a fag hag, so I started doing the girl thing. I felt that girls were safer than guys. But I didn't like sex with them any more than I liked sex with guys, so I had to get drunker to do it. The emotional support I got from having sex with women was much better. At that time, I had no boundaries when it came to sex. My body had been taken and abused for four years through incest. The only emotional support I got from my family was through food, money, gifts or incest. I called myself "trisexual" because I would try anything sexual—from women to men—my closet door was revolving. It was impossible for me to maintain a long-term relationship with anyone.

Looking back on those years, I had a lot of shame about it. I've done a lot of therapy and a lot of work on myself. Now I'm very grateful I never got pregnant out of wedlock or got any sexually transmitted diseases, other than venereal disease of the eye. I'm very grateful that I never did any permanent damage to myself or to other people. I took my relationships seriously whenever I was lucky enough to be in one. I never had sex out of marriage. I may have been a promiscuous, but whenever I was in a committed relationship, I had integrity. I wouldn't mess around on anybody.

What I've seen so many times in my practice as a therapist is that many women who have been sexually violated and begin lesbian relationships aren't really lesbians at all but are turning away from men and their history of abuse at men's hands. Weight gain and obesity are often a result of sexual abuse. It doesn't quite make sense logically, but at a subconscious level, people build a protective barrier around themselves to protect themselves from abuse, also making themselves as unattractive as possible.

After I left Dale I went to Northern California for a spiritual retreat. After it was over I was to stay in a hotel in San Francisco and do some post-retreat writing. Some of my friends from the retreat were staying nearby. It happened to be Gay Pride Weekend. This was before I came out with my new sexual orientation. No one in my family—a family that looked good—had the slightest idea that I was dating girls. Even though I had committed at the retreat to do certain spiritual exercises, I thought, "Here I am in San Francisco during Pride, the biggest place for it, a once-in-a-lifetime opportunity. I should try to enjoy myself." To hell with spiritual exercises, I was on my way to the dyke parade!

My friends and I rented a limousine, got into the middle of this dyke parade, and picked up a bunch of girls to ride in the limousine with us. We started drinking and before long, our shirts and bras were flying off our skins. Standing topless through the sunroof of the limousine and cheering, we were having a blast. Nobody was even looking at us because the street was filled with naked people. It was fun and I felt so free!

My mom called me up a few days later and asked if I had been to San Francisco, and I said yes. She asked, "Did you go to Gay Pride?" I was like, "Oh no!" But I summoned the courage to utter a cautious "Yes." And she said, "I think I saw you on TV." Yikes! My heart started pounding and I got this lump in my throat. I was thinking, "Please tell me, Mother, you did NOT see me standing topless out of a limo." She asked, "Were you wearing a white shirt?" "Oh no, that wasn't me," I quickly replied. What a relief! If she had asked, "Were you topless?" we would have had a different conversation. But here I was, almost forty years old, a successful therapist and a mother of two children, and I was still terrified of my mother! It says a lot about the power my parents had over me.

Through all that stuff, dating men, dating women, and being "trisexual," I finally realized that I needed to harmonize the various parts of me. I couldn't be one way with one group and then be another way with another group. The secrecy and shame were killing me. I would have to embrace all of me and present all of me to people, and they would have to make a choice, to take it or leave it. Eventually, I divorced my husband and was dating women exclusively. A wise woman once told me, "Until you are totally happy with who you are, don't get in a relationship, because you will attract who you really are." She went on, "When you have self-esteem issues, which you do, you feel like shit. You think butterflies are attracted to shit? No! Flies are attracted to shit." I took her advice and spent eleven years single, most of that time dating women. I eventually came out to my parents about my sexuality. I believed I was bisexual but I knew my parents wouldn't understand that, so I told them I was gay. My father's response was, "I don't care who you sleep with as long as you are happy and don't let people take advantage of you." My mother's response was, "Why are you telling us this now? Are you moving somebody in with you?" My response was, "Gee, no, Mama, I just am tired of living a lie and thought you might like to know who your daughter really is."

My Second Husband, Bill

About a year before I met Bill, I felt I had learned all I could from being in relationships with women. It was time for me to face my demons and try to be in a relationship with a man again. I had realized my attempts to be in a relationship with women were based in needs rooted in looking for mothering as well as running from my earlier sexual abuses by men. I decided to open myself up to the possibility of a relationship with a man, but I had no idea where to look. I was a single parent, and all I did at the time was work as a therapist, go to AA meetings, and make round trips to my kids' school. That was essentially my life. I wasn't going to date any of my clients and I wasn't going to date any of my AA friends. The guys at my kids' school were a bunch of rednecks, so that wasn't an option. I had no way of meeting anybody and couldn't figure out a way to put myself back on the market.

I had dated a few men in AA, but the catches in AA are not very good. They're often sociopathic or, at best, disturbed. I'd already done that. I had met my first husband at AA and you already know how that turned out. I talked to my sponsor, asking her what to do about meeting a guy: that's what you do in

Expect a Miracle

AA, you go to your sponsor with your problems. She suggested placing an ad on Yahoo Personals, and that's what I did. I wrote a pretty tough ad. Not too many men would be attracted to it. But I did that on purpose, to filter out the riffraff. I had learned from working with sex offenders that the internet is 35 percent pornography and that's where most of them had gotten their start. That made me leery about dating through the internet. I reconsidered after my father called me up and said, "You're not going to believe who's on Match.com." Here's my father, seventy-six years old, just learning how to surf the Internet. He said, "Your brother." And I said, "Bill's on Match.com?" "Yeah," he said. "Well, I've got to check this out," I told him. I had never even looked at the personals before. That was six years ago and the internet wasn't anything like it is today. There weren't many success stories about couples meeting on the internet because most were long distance. I looked at my brother's ad, and I thought, "Well, if there are people of his caliber on here, there might be someone out there for me."

I believe there is a spiritual consciousness to the internet. I began to pray for the Creator to bring the person for me into my life via the internet. I took a spiritual approach when I wrote my ad and decided to meet only local people. I said that I wanted to find somebody whom I was physically, emotionally, spiritually, and intellectually compatible with, a person with whom I could communicate, be comfortable, and trust. These were all necessary ingredients for me in a relationship. I probably met four or five guys before Bill. And they were all really nice guys. One of them was more interested in me than I was in him, and one I was more interested in than he was in me.

Bill lived right across town. I didn't respond to his email at first because I had just been diagnosed with breast cancer and was undergoing treatment. You don't think about dating anybody when you've just had breast surgery. But he was persistent. I eventually responded and said, "You know, there's some stuff going on in my life right now. The timing just isn't good." He said, "Why? Have you got breast cancer?" Astonished, I said, "Yes, I do." He said, "That's ok, I survived Hodgkin's lymphoma, and had only a 35 percent chance of living. I was on chemo and radiation for six months. I can help you. At least come have coffee with me." I did, and it was love at first sight for both of us.

I was anxious to know what had happened in his last relationship because I think that we tend to repeat our patterns, especially if we never received any type of help in letting go of the underlying issues. Bill had never been to therapy. He didn't understand why anybody would waste their time going to therapy. In fact, he was outright anti-therapy, as I later discovered. He was skeptical about many of the things I believed in—tarot cards, counseling, and spirituality—yet he was somewhat curious about them.

Anyway, I sent him an email, asking him what happened in his marriage. I can still see that instant message box on my computer screen. He wrote back: "One day my wife came home, picked up and packed up and left, telling me she needed to find herself. That night, she moved in with her boss who was a lesbian, so I guess she had a pretty good compass. I actually like her better as a lesbian. Maybe there's a toaster oven in here for somebody." I liked his sense of humor. Little did he know that I had just quit dating women—how synchronistic! I decided to give him a chance.

Being the scaredy cat that I was, I met him downtown in a public place for coffee, and when he got out of the Jeep, it was love at first sight. I know he knew it. We sat at a corner table at the Common Grounds coffee shop on Dickson Street in Fayetteville, Arkansas talking all day, completely absorbed in each other. It was difficult for us to pull ourselves apart. We could have easily spent a night at the coffee shop if they were open all night. It was the first time in my life that I lost track of time sober. That was on New Year's Day of 2005—what a way to start the year! Six months later, we were married. We celebrated our sixth wedding anniversary on July 2, 2011. Everything happened so fast. He moved in fast, we married fast, and I was fast to start perfecting my skills in reading the cards. I wanted to prepare myself to better understand relationships and have the tools to help me do everything I can to make sure our marriage works and to help other couples in my counseling practice.

As a seasoned therapist specializing in addictions, trauma, and codependency, the intensity between Bill and me excited and terrified me at the same time. I was afraid I was entering yet another codependent relationship. It was my mindset that this intensity and sense of knowing each other already might be pathological. At the time, I was an amateur astrologist. It's one of the tools I used in my practice. I had also opened up to psychic awareness after having practiced meditation for several years. I knew Bill and I weren't compatible astrologically. So I went online and found someone who could do a psychic reading. I said, "I already know we're not astrologically compatible, so don't do that." She sent me a twenty-page reading utilizing a deck of playing cards.

My cancer was discovered by a spiritual medium, Sharlette Pumphrey. She had done readings for me off and on for several years with considerable accuracy and had become a good friend. One night I had tremendous pains in my lower abdomen, so bad I thought I would have to go to the hospital. When I called my doctor the next day he couldn't see me for three weeks because he was going out of town. I called Sharlette to ask her what she thought I should do. She did a reading and said she saw what looked like an English pea, and interpreted it as cancer—ovarian cancer, I guess, because of the shape of the pea and the fact that the pain was in my lower abdomen. When I went to the doctor and told him I had ovarian cancer, he chastised me for doing too much reading on the internet and recommended a mammogram. He did examine my ovaries and they seemed fine. I hadn't had a mammogram in ten years because I didn't believe in them. After having the mammogram and biopsy, the radiologist called me in to show me my X-ray. As he pointed to the tumor on the screen, his words were, "Do you see that spot there that looks like an English pea?" This experience further advanced my spiritual and metaphysical quest.

Bill and I read the reading the psychic did for me and were quite impressed and validated with her explanation of the nature of our relationship. It explained the intense attraction and depth

Expect a Miracle

of love from a spiritual perspective. It showed us what we are here to do for each other, and together, for the world, as well as how best to utilize the connections between us. It explained our connections in terms of past lives, a concept that was new and questionable for both of us. It turned out the reader had used the Cards of Destiny from the Order of the Magi. Intrigued by her report, I started studying the cards with a wise lady from New York City, Leslie Ahmed. She was my mentor for several years. I learned so much about life and the cards from her and she was a tremendous source of education and support. I began doing readings for clients and was featured on the local news as a psychic. It was a big step for me to come out on the news as a psychic because I had built a successful private practice on traditional psychotherapy based on science! From the destiny cards, I went into clairvoyant training and from there into shamanic studies.

Eight

Marriage and Step-parenting

"LIKE IT OR NOT, EVERYTHING IS CHANGING. The result will be the most wonderful experience in the history of man or the most horrible enslavement that you can imagine. Be active or abdicate. The future is in your hands."

— WILLIAM COOPER

By the time Bill and I got married, I had been a practicing psychotherapist for sixteen years. I did not have many clients who had issues with stepparenting, so I had no experience directly or indirectly in stepparenting. I barely knew how to be a mother, let alone a stepmother. When Bill and I met, our idea was to combine our families. Bill brought the younger of his two sons and his daughter into the marriage. His younger son was twenty-one and his daughter was nineteen. I brought in my son, Clay, age sixteen, and daughter, Molly, age fourteen. I had this storybook idea of how all of us would become one big happy family with everyone getting his and her needs met. Bill would love my kids the way he loves his, and I would love

Expect a Miracle

his kids the way I love mine. His kids would establish a close relationship with me and my kids with him, and the kids would come to us for guidance, we would all hang out together and be one big happy family, with Peter Pan and Tinker Bell and the magic dust and all of that. To be blunt, it was a nightmare.

While Bill and I were still dating, he expressed concerns about some problems his ex-wife had. He really wanted me to be able to give his kids something they had never had before. He saw me as somebody who could do that, and I wanted Bill to do the same for my kids, who had not had a male figure in their lives since they were toddlers. My kids were still living at home with me. His kids were older and more independent.

We wanted Bill's daughter to move in with us, but she wanted her father to stay with her, separate from me and my kids. I tried to help Bill's kids by giving them books on how to handle their mother. They confided in me about her. I was hoping to help them better understand her, but I think I may have gone overboard. I tried too hard, and in so doing, I pushed them away. I called myself a "stepmonster," instead of stepmother, because nothing I did had been right with two out of Bill's three kids. It wasn't easy with my kids either. My kids had been raised by me, a pretty easygoing, flexible woman, and they had never known a man in the house. Their father and I split when they were just two and four, so they'd never lived with a man. And here comes a former drill sergeant, very consistent, very patient. They alternated between loving and hating him. For the first couple of years, they called him "Sergeant Asshole." At one point they went and bought him a license plate for the front of his truck.

It said: Drill sergeant. Bill was actually a drill sergeant in the army until his retirement a few years before we met. He was very successful with my kids because he was able to see more potential in my kids than I did.

There wasn't much good literature about stepparenting back then and probably this is still true now. I just want to say to those people who are doing it: "Hang in there!" Understand that it's very difficult. Second marriages are difficult anyway, even if you don't have kids. And then you start adding kids to the mix and you have your kids and his kids and our kids. Bill and I don't have any biological kids together, but I've seen that problem in therapy. Because then the stepkids think that the kids you have together are more favored than they are. I just think stepparenting is difficult. Being a stepchild is difficult too because children, even as they grow into young adults, often do not want to see their parents with another person. They want to see their parents together, forever! And it's very hard to see somebody coming in and loving that parent, and having a physical relationship with that person, and accepting that person into that family. And in some ways, it's harder for them the older they get. It's a bit easier when they are much younger.

The most important thing is to figure out how to develop a team between the husband and the wife and be on solid ground. That's the base camp for the family. Then, if the husband and wife are a team and cannot be split by the kids, the husband and wife have a better chance of unifying the family. We did not do that and I believe that's the reason our family suffered.

Expect a Miracle

As a spouse and a stepparent, you have to build up your new spouse to your own kids, but not to the point where they start resenting it. And you don't want to praise the stepparent/spouse over their biological mother or father. Another important consideration is, when you leave your child's parent, make sure you do not degrade that parent to the children. That is a costly mistake we both have made. While it may be true that your ex was a jerk, it does no good to say that to your kids. It's best that you share the fine qualities of your ex with your kids. No matter how horrible a person is, he or she does have one or two admirable qualities. Emphasize those qualities to the kids! By doing so, you'll be helping the kids build a great self-esteem and emotional stability.

One of the things I learned in premarital counseling with Brother Ed, before my first husband and I got married, was that everybody needs supervision and help in a marriage. Whether stepkids are involved or not, marriage is one of the hardest things we do. In all of his years as a Methodist minister, Brother Ed had never seen a marriage that could not be saved if there was help early enough. So, always find an objective party as soon as you think you need it. Don't wait until you're ready for a divorce. Let go of your pride and ego and be willing to go for help as early as possible.

Now, what if your partner is resisting outside help? Well, first you ask him or her again to reconsider going for help. Then plead with your partner to help save the relationship in which you have both invested so much. If that doesn't work, then it's time for you to set your boundary: Let's get help or it's over!

In all my years of counseling, there's something I've learned about men. We women can be so nagging that men just tune out.

They stop listening even though it might seem like they are paying attention. It reminds me of the Far Side cartoon where the man is yelling at the dog and all the dog hears is his name and Blah blah blah. But then, men are willing to do something different once the wife's out the door, when she says, "I'm done. I'm leaving you," and she actually leaves. At that point, most men become bewildered. They often can't believe she really meant what she was saying.

There's that old joke that says, "How many therapists does it take to change a light bulb?" One, but the light bulb really has to want to change. You can't make your husband or wife want to make the marriage work. But you can set the boundaries: If you don't go for help, I'm going to leave. Be firm about it because it's your life that your partner is dealing with. You can never recover the years you've spent in any relationship, good or bad. So, if they are not willing to save the relationship, you may just have to move on.

Now, I have to say that setting boundaries with a man does not always work. Men often see such boundaries as ultimatums and may become resistant. It really boils down to how much they value the relationship. Recently I went through a situation with my husband. I used the boundary method and he rebuffed it. So, I decided that I am here to love him no matter what he is doing. He's not messing around on me. The stuff he does is pretty minor in the big scheme of things. I can't make him see my perspective unless he wants to. And I can't make him change. That's his choice. All I can change is me, and usually that is hard enough.

I believe Bill and I are twin flames. Twin flames are also called soul twins and, unlike soul mates, where a person may have many, we each only have one twin flame. This is not to say we are not complete souls in ourselves, because we are. Together we bring two complete, balanced male and female souls to the picture. Many people seem to yearn for this reunion and I can understand why. It is profoundly intimate. Yet it is far from easy. We challenge each other daily on every level of our being. It has been hard work, yet we have landed in a place of bliss and unconditional love and regard for each other.

As I said earlier, when I put out my personal ad, I said that I wanted someone whom I was emotionally, intellectually, physically, and spiritually compatible with, with whom I could communicate, be comfortable with, and trust. And I've learned from reading the cards that when men are courting, they will tell a woman just about anything. They say, "Okay, so she wants me to be this, so I'll be that." This is especially true of younger men. That's just a part of who men are. Some women are like that, too! They can justify anything. We all try to look good when we are courting, and the real person doesn't come out until the marriage license is signed and registered down at the courthouse.

Bill has done more spiritual growth in the last six years that we've been married than most people do in a lifetime. He's a wise man. We're all spiritual beings on our unique journeys. It's just a matter of when each person is ready to begin their conscious journey. I think that if both partners are doing work on themselves, the relationship, like wine, improves as it ages.

Nine

The Drill Sergeant Worked Wonders with My Kids

> "Our greatest duty and our main responsibility is to help others. But please, if you can't help them, would you please not hurt them."
>
> — Dalai Lama

When my husband, Bill, came on the scene, he wasted no time in helping straighten out my out-of-control children. He had trained in Interactive Metronome (IM) and he used the technique to revolutionize the lives of my two kids, Clay and Molly, then sixteen and fourteen years old, respectively. Interactive Metronome is an assessment and treatment tool used in therapy to improve the way the brain functions. It provides a structured, goal-oriented process that challenges the patient to synchronize a range of hand and foot exercises to a precise computer-generated reference tone heard through headphones. The patient attempts to match the rhythmic beat with repetitive motor actions. A visual-sound guidance system provides immediate feedback measured in milliseconds, and a score is provided. Over the course of the treatment, patients learn to focus and attend for longer periods of time, increase physical endurance and stamina, filter out internal and external distractions, improve ability to monitor mental and physical actions as they are occurring, and progressively improve coordinated performance. IM is often used to treat patients suffering from sensory integration disorder, ADD/ADHD, traumatic brain injury (TBI), cerebral vascular accident (CVA), autism spectrum disorder, cerebral palsy, Parkinson's disease, and other conditions that affect the nervous system.

Clay was evaluated by his school's psychologist before and after Bill put him through Interactive Metronome. Clay demonstrated marked neurological dysfunctions before IM. After a series of exercises with IM, his evaluation showed no dysfunction at all. My son, Clay, had skated through his whole life. Everything had always been done for him. Believe it or not, I brushed his teeth for him until he was thirteen years old. Finally I refused to do it anymore; I couldn't do it. It would be insane on my part to continue promoting that kind of laziness. Clay had this "learned helplessness" that had worked for him. I remember taking him to Wal-Mart when he was about ten years old and being appalled by something he said. He saw some fat, perhaps handicapped, customers driving around in motorized carts, and said, "Mom, when I grow up, I want to be just like them. That way, I won't ever have to walk again." Now, that was different. Usually kids want to grow up to be a fireman, doctor, pilot, and so on. My kid wanted to ride in a motorized cart. Internally choked up by emotions, I didn't know what to say. As he grew up, I didn't have much in the way of expectations for him.

Many experts predicted Clay would never drive, finish high school, or even go to college. The general assumption was that he'd never do anything with his life. They condemned my hopes for him and expectations of him and sadly, I gave in. Bill would not accept that. He saw potential in the kid and knew he was only sandbagging—acting like he can't do anything. In his four years as a drill sergeant, Bill saw many guys like Clay who did a great job at hiding their potential.

He took Clay on because he loved the kid and because he loved me, too. He took on Molly, too. He has helped make them what they are today. Clay can drive because Bill taught him to drive. He gave Clay his Jeep, a car that was very special to Bill. In his senior year of high school, Clay got off the Individualized Education Plan, a special program for slow students, and did his school work without help for the first time since the second grade. For the first time in his life, he got a job. His first jobs weren't anything great, but it was a remarkable accomplishment. He initially worked at fast food chains. Not enjoying that work, he applied for a job at the local psychiatric hospital to be a psych technician, working with kids. He's been doing that for over two years. He understands and cares about these kids because of all he has been through. He has struggled. His early childhood was not easy, with his father not being there, and he has had drug and alcohol problems. When we first moved to Kauai, he came with me and was able to get off drugs. So he's doing well. He even looks like me now, poor kid.

My daughter, Molly, entered this world ready to rule a small planet. She's the baby of the family but you would never know it. She's two years younger than Clay. He was born in 1987 and she was born in 1989. They have the same astrological sign—Sun and Mercury both in Taurus, and I wonder, "What did I do in a past life to deserve this?" By nature, the Taurus is stubborn and slow. Since Taurus is slow and Mercury is the mind, the individual with Mercury in Taurus will be slow to make up their mind. So my kids are stubborn and they don't do anything quick. I say they have two speeds: slow and stop. Being a Gemini, I demanded the Gemini life out of them, which was constant changing and what they saw as inconsistency. I'm sure they hated that, but being Tauruses they are patient and loyal.

In the cards I do, Molly's the king of clubs. My friend is an evolutionary astrologist and he tells me Molly was a king of a corrupt army in her past life. She'd tried to get them to go straight, and they wouldn't. She tried and she tried, and finally she joined them. And her challenge this time is to not join the corrupt army, to stay a good leader. She came out very psychic and strong in her sense of self. To this day, my sense of self is nowhere near Molly's.

At the age of two, when her father and I were splitting up, I was tying Molly's shoes, and her father was being verbally abusive to me. She turned around, looked at him, and yelled, "Get outta here, we don't need you!" She also did that when I broke up with a boyfriend when she was four. She said, "Get out of here, we don't need you." As I have shared here, her father would disappear for weeks at a time, hitting up emergency rooms to get drugs, going to hospitals and faking kidney stones to get drugs. Every time he'd leave, she'd know it. Even at age two, she'd tell me, "He's getting ready to leave." I would say "No, no, he's not going to leave," because I didn't want to believe it. But she was always right.

She was a "nature kid," for she never wanted to wear clothes. We moved to California when she was five. She would go to kindergarten and start taking off her clothes on her way to class. Then she started pushing around the other kids. Her teacher finally came up to me and said, "Your daughter is a bully. She's mean to the other students. If you don't do something now, she's not going to have any empathy for anybody." So I got her into therapy at the age of five so that she could learn empathy.

At the suggestion of the school and experts, I held Clay back from first grade to give him more time to mature. When he was in first grade, Molly was in kindergarten, and she had to grow up in the shadow of a brother who was always doing weird stuff. Everyone was always saying, "Your brother is weird." "He's weird." She had to grow up under somebody who had very socially unacceptable behavior for Southern California. If we had gone back to Arkansas, up in the hills, he would have fit right in. Californians were skaters or surfers. Clay was heavyset and clumsy and just wasn't into that stuff. Until he had brain gym therapy years later, he couldn't balance on a skateboard.

Expect a Miracle

Molly, on the other hand, was like an actress, very beautiful and very concerned with the way she looked and how everything appears. And here was her brother, a slob who doesn't care about anything. So she was terribly embarrassed by him; she was also embarrassed by me. Most significantly, she was embarrassed by her father, a drug addict who was in and out of prison. You know, for all her adolescent life, she was embarrassed of her family. She was embarrassed by me for being a lesbian. She'd get attached to my girlfriends and they'd leave. And now here she is with a girl. Karma! She claims she's not a lesbian, though, and adds, "If it doesn't work out with my current girlfriend, I'll go back to guys." She knows the relationship is about the soul, not the body.

Bill coming into our lives was a real blessing. For the first time ever, we had a protector. We had family. And Bill and I were a family. Bill saved my kids, and he saved me. My kids were really taxing me. They were fourteen and sixteen and fighting all the time. Mostly it was Molly fighting Clay. She was a little dictator. She physically abused him constantly. I would say, "Clay, you've got to fight back, you've got to take care of yourself. Hit her or whatever." And he would just cry, "I can't hurt her, Mom, I can't hurt her," and he wouldn't hurt her. So she continued taking out her frustrations on him. It was tough, but they're getting all that worked out now. But it was tough. I mean, I had to hold the door to keep her from coming in and doing damage. She was very aggressive. She made multiple holes in the wall. In fact, she ended up spending most of her life with no door in her room. When she didn't knock down the door, you can rest assured there was no doorknob on the door. She had no respect for boundaries, including other people's boundaries.

Bill and I had just gotten married and were going on our honeymoon, to stay at my parents' condo in Hot Springs, Arkansas. We had to take her along because we had nobody to take care of her. She sat outside our bedroom door on the night of our honeymoon. "Let me in, let me in, let me in," she screamed. So we had to take her into the bed with us, and that was our whole honeymoon. She was fourteen.

When we sent her to rehab, she would come home with new tricks, just like when my son went to camp and there were kids with Asperger's and Tourette's syndrome—he'd come home acting like he had Tourette's. He didn't have it, but he was walking around saying "Cock-a-doodle-doo!" Molly got back from rehab and had learned how to cut. She started cutting herself and it was pretty bloody. In one instance, she locked herself in a closet, and Bill and I were standing next to the closet pleading with her to come out. She screamed, "Don't you come in here! Don't you come in here!" Bill demanded, "Your mother and I are both mandated reporters, so we're going to have to call Family Services if you don't let us in there." She peeked through the closet door, looked at Bill, and said, "If you come near me, I'll tell them you raped me." She didn't like Bill at first. In fact, she wouldn't even get in the car with him, and that wasn't just because she didn't like him, but also because she was afraid of men in general. We had filed a FINS petition on her for Family Services because she was completely out of control. This basically meant that Bill and I were with her in the house for a year. She couldn't go anywhere without us. A FINS (Family In Need of Services) petition is filed in court on a juvenile over ten years old, who is: habitually and without justification absent from school while subject to compulsory school attendance; habitually disobedient to the reasonable and lawful commands of the parents, guardians, or custodian; absent from home without sufficient cause, permission, or justification; and in need of counseling or other services. Under the provisions of FINS, a judge can order family services or place the juvenile in a treatment facility if testimony shows a need for this placement.

The court does not place juveniles into a facility unless an assessment recommends that the juvenile needs treatment. The judge can also place the juvenile in the Juvenile Detention Center for not following the judge's orders. In certain cases, the judge can order a transfer of the juvenile's custody. Family Services provides relevant services including, but not limited to random drug screens, drug and alcohol treatment, counseling, family therapy, and psychological evaluations. Essentially, Family Services are provided in order to assist the family in getting necessary help for the juvenile and his/her family (counseling, drug and alcohol treatment, etc.).

Two years later, she moved to Kauai, Hawaii with Bill and me. When I think back to the way she used to be, it's almost like waking up from a nightmare. She has since left Kauai and returned to Arkansas to find her own path and become more independent. She enrolled in school to become a CNA and later went to work in a nursing home, but she didn't like it. She decided to go to beauty school but dropped out. She's outstanding in everything she does, but she won't stick with it. She could have been an Olympic-level athlete in any sport if she tried. She's beautiful. She could be a model. She's funny. She's loyal. She's smart but she's stubborn. She is waiting tables in Arkansas, gaining knowledge in her off-hours at Barnes and Noble, and contemplating going back to school in the fall. So she's on her path and trying to find her way. You know, it's hard for girls with strong mothers like me. In her earlier years, she almost killed herself. She was homeless for two years. She has had a tough path, like my son. But I think she's really on track now.

Bill has had a rough time being a part of our family, but he stepped up to the plate because he believes in my kids and loves them. He's our angel. I would like to be able to provide Bill's children with the same kind of support. I have done and will continue to do my best.

Ten

The Temporality of Life

A MOTHER IS A PERSON WHO SEEING THERE ARE ONLY FOUR PIECES OF PIE FOR FIVE PEOPLE, promptly announces she never did care for pie.

— Tenneva Jordan

Following the recent death of my mother, I thought a lot about the temporality of life and the many ways in which we react or respond to the passing of a loved one. I wanted to include a chapter about my thoughts on death and dying because it is another subject that people try to avoid, yet it is a natural part of life, in fact, an inescapable part of life. And frankly, many people don't know how to deal with it, especially when it involves someone close to them. The following are my thoughts on the subject.

It seems to me that Western culture has dealt with death and dying by avoiding the issue and turning away from it. Even when confronted with it personally with somebody close dying, people often just want it over with and to get on with their lives. Although a natural part of life, it is misunderstood and ignored. Children are curious about it and are often shielded from the truth. People might call me morbid, but I have always been fascinated with death. I remember in the second grade when my beloved great-aunt died, my mother wouldn't let me attend her funeral because she said I was too young. I was upset and saddened by her decision. What I have learned through the years is that each person deals with life and death from their own state of consciousness, and states of consciousness can vary considerably within families.

The first funerals I attended were those of my grandparents. I loved them dearly and the loss was significant. There wasn't much drama that impacted me. The distribution of assets was prearranged and it was done in a very orderly, civil fashion. We grandchildren had a lot of fun connecting with each other, socializing and sharing stories. I remember our parents chastising us for laughing too loudly, because they didn't want friends who were bringing food by to think we weren't grieving. When my mother's mother died, many of my family had tickets to an Elvis concert and we had plans for dressing up for the concert and really having a ball. Our mothers were opposed to us going to the concert, but eventually relented if we promised to go in a low-key fashion. To me death is cause for celebration, and I just didn't understand their level of consciousness at the time that would see it otherwise.

I view life as eternal and see death as only the loss of the physical body. The soul gets to soar on to what I believe are more joyous experiences, especially if the body has begun to suffer or deteriorate. I also believe we choose our own time so I believe the newly deceased are fine although I do believe that prayers and rituals help them with their transitions. The sadness is for those left behind and their loss.

Just before my mother died recently, she confirmed this. As my husband and I sat beside her bed in the hospital in Arkansas, one day she was in and out of consciousness. Death is a process, not an event, and I believe it can begin long before the soul leaves the body. Mama opened her eyes and looked at me and said: "Have you met a lady from South Carolina?" My mouth dropped open and my husband I looked at each other stunned. I replied, "As a matter of fact, I have; two of my best friends on Kauai are from South Carolina and I recently met their mother who lives in South Carolina." There is no way she could have known that unless she had been with me on Kauai. Another example occurred after I went back to our home in Winslow. I called to check on her and she got on the phone and asked me where I was. When I told her Winslow she asked me if I had gotten my problems straightened out there. Again, something she never would have known had she not been with me in Winslow.

I shared these stories with my youngest brother, Stuart, and he shared similar experiences. While he found them eerie, I found them comforting. It confirmed to me that we exist on many planes inside and outside the body and life is eternal. I carry this with me on a daily basis.

A local Hawaiian man told me recently that his father compared parents' deaths to the death of the tree and the offspring the roots of the tree. He said that when the tree dies, the roots go nuts. Some people have shared with me their belief that when a parent dies the adult children return to their original behaviors as children in the family. Another person said they become even more obvious versions of who they really are. The latter has been my experience and also relates back to my earlier statement that people react related to their current level of consciousness. It also appears that the roles the parents play and which parent dies first also matter, in addition to the particular dynamics of the family.

My family was patriarchal, very much controlled by Father until his death. All of my brothers worked for him and two of my brothers have rarely worked for anybody but him. All of us have been and still are involved in family businesses together. My father used money to control us and keep us where he wanted us. When he died the control was gone; money and assets and care of our elderly mother remained. The dance our family had done for many years lost the lead dancer and the family had to learn to dance without him. We all did our best but there were many horrifying events that occurred and we each reacted to the loss not only from our own perceptions and levels of consciousness, but from the relationship we had with our father.

It had been a long time since we were a close family, so instead of pulling together as some families do, we pulled apart. Various alignments between siblings were formed at different times for different reasons but never for any length of time. My brothers are all more focused on the material world than I am. My focus for many years has been on spirituality, and while I have engaged in petty fights with them from time to time, I have always sought their forgiveness and granted them mine unasked.

The loss of the head of the family left everybody scrambling for position but for the most part my oldest brother stepped in. The fact that my mother remained alive and somewhat aware kept some order, but not enough. My brothers controlled the care of my mother until her death, which has been very hard for me, her only daughter, to accept. My mother and I were never close, but I wanted to do right by her, ensure that my father's wishes for her were respected, and give her an end of this life that she wanted and that I would want for her. My youngest brother seemed to want the same for her, especially toward the end, but we were only two voices in a system where majority ruled. The only way I have been able to deal with this is to accept that my mother chose to stay in her hometown and at some level this must either have been her choice or karma.

When my father was dying his body was ill but his mind was sharp until the end. His process took a short five weeks. In contrast, my mother's death process took over twenty years, beginning with her cerebral aneurysm. That was when I truly lost my mother, the one I had grown up with and knew forever.

Expect a Miracle

The aneurysm left her with a whole new personality. I had to grieve the mother I had known and accept the replacement. Fortunately she and my father did it with grace and humor, never burdening their children with anything. I had the opportunity to make peace with my parents over the past and come together in a new, closer relationship. My father and I enjoyed a close relationship like we had never had before. I suspect that was due to my mother and her jealousy over me, but I can't be sure. After her aneurysm she was much like a child and a very different person for a long time.

My mother began a rapid decline in January of 2011 and expressed that she was ready to go. She told me there were many things worse than death. I was trying to get sitters for her because I was not content with the care provided for her in her nursing home and had finally gotten my brothers to agree. When my father died in 2007 he wanted around-the-clock care for her and she and my brothers resisted. I told my mother that if she was ready to leave Earth School, she still had lessons to learn and had to learn to receive to graduate. She allowed us to hire sitters, whom she quickly came to rely upon and love. All of her sitters for the last nine months were wonderful loving black women. She, like me, felt safer and more loved by them. Mossie Nesby and Rena Clark were her two main sitters and I couldn't have moved to Kauai nor made it through her death without them. I love them as much as she did. She said she felt like she was being treated like a newborn baby. Her death ended the short-lived matriarchy of our family and the final cutting of the umbilical cord.

My brothers and I all reacted to her death from our various states of consciousness. One of my brothers avoided it and was ready to move on. Another brother was angry and vicious, acting as if he was my mother's only child. Yet, my other brother was trying to keep the peace and show respect, realizing that Mother was dying all along and doing whatever was possible to ease the transition. Some families come close at times like these. Ours did not. I wrote about this to share the various experiences that are possible during the passing of a key family member, like the father or mother. You can't expect the same reaction from each family member. Each will react according to level of understanding or state of awareness and temperament. So, be open to the various ways in which your family members may react to the inevitable passing of your parents and try not to hold it against them, for it is the only way they know to deal with such an event.

Eleven

A Refusal to Give Up

"Keep on going, and the chances are that you will stumble on something, perhaps when you are least expecting it. I never heard of anyone ever stumbling on something sitting down."

— Charles F. Kettering

As I was thinking about this theme of refusing to give up, my mind took me all the way back to fourth grade. That was when the incest started. I remember that my classmates, especially girls, were making fun of me. They were teasing me because I was getting myself into a lot of trouble in school. I got caught cheating on an achievement test in school and wet my pants. I got into a fight with a boy on the playground. As if that wasn't enough, I got caught in the bathroom comparing pubic hairs with an older girl and the school called my mother and sent me home. So the fourth grade was a horrible year for me, but I never gave up.

My best friend in school from kindergarten till grade school was Virginia. Her mother and my mother were good friends, and our grandmothers were good friends. She lived within walking distance and we played together almost every day after school for years. She was more of a follower; I was not. She hung out with, and gave her allegiance to, the Queen Bee of our school, Beth. The term Queen Bee usually refers to the head bee in a bee hive but in this sense it refers to the most popular girl in the crowd: where she led, many followed. After high school she hooked up with a local hippie and became a member of Hare Krishna. They went to India and her parents had to get help from the U.S. State Department to get her out of India. But during my time with her, she was a threat to anyone she didn't like. She could and would sic the popular crowd on you if she had a bone to pick with you. In the fourth grade I was her victim. She got the popular crowd, including my best friend, to ignore and deny my existence. They acted as if I was invisible. I walked up to Virginia and asked her what was going on and she acted as if I weren't there. When other friends of mine would ask one of them why they were doing this, they would respond with: "Who is Marianne?" This was my first experience with shunning and feeling unseen. Fortunately I had never been one to just hang with the click of popular girls. I had friends from many different groups and I continued to hang out with them, but the scar was left by my best friend choosing to follow the crowd at my expense. Even with this shunning, I dusted myself off, got up, and went about the task of developing new friendships.

Then when my parents sent me off to the mental institution, word got out that I had been sent off because I was pregnant. I had been sent to an unwed mothers' home. I would come home and everyone would be talking about me being in a mental institution. And my mother's friends, not close friends, but some of the society ladies would ask me questions like, "And where are you now?" looking at me suspiciously. I always wanted to say, "Well, my parents had me chained up in the attic and they just let me out for the weekend." But I wouldn't. I'd say that "I'm living in North Carolina, going to school."

In my town, you didn't speak the truth. It was a looking-good-and-feeling-bad town. I remember during my senior year in a public high school in Arkansas, I enrolled in a psychology class and because of my experiences I knew more about it than the teacher did. I challenged her ideas. One day she had the guidance counselor call me out of class. I had a nice visit with the guidance counselor but couldn't really understand the purpose of our meeting. When I went back to class one of my friends leaned over to me and told me that the teacher had informed the class to humor me but not to feed into me because I had "problems" and that I had been diagnosed as "maniac depressive." The diagnostic category was manic depressive, and although many of my family members had been diagnosed with this debilitating disorder, I had not. I was ashamed and humiliated; on disclosing this to my parents, we decided that I should go back to the mental institution to finish high school. Even then, I didn't give up, I just changed the plan.

Expect a Miracle

Because I had been institutionalized for such a long time in a controlled environment, I did not know how to live in the outside world. I didn't know how to deal with feelings, freedom, and choices. Decision making was out, as it had always been done for me, and learning to live by my own truth was out as well because the truth of the various authority figures in my life overruled mine. They told me when to go to bed and when to get up. If I was happy, they gave me tranquilizers. If I was sad, they give me antidepressants. There were advantages to this kind of life. It was easy. Very little was required of me and the expectations were low. But the loss of self and liberty was far more debilitating than I knew as a teenager, yet I kept on going.

Diagnosed chronically mentally ill at a young age and destined for a life as an "ironing lady," I refused to accept that definition of me. I was told that I was too stupid to go to college and that I was not capable of having a career and needed to learn a trade or skill. I refused to accept that definition of me, too.

I had applied for college in North Carolina, took the SATs, didn't do very well on those kinds of tests. My score was miserably low, yet I got in. When I declared my major, Ted, head of the psychology department at the time, looked at my SAT scores and told me that I was lucky to be admitted into the college. He said, "You are going to have to work hard." Well, I was doing a lot of drinking and drugging during college, and in my first psych class I learned about state-dependent learning. If you are drinking when you are studying, you'd better be drinking when you taking the test. If you are smoking dope when you're studying, you'd better be smoking dope when you take the test. So once I got that coordinated, I did pretty well. It took me ten years, but I didn't give up. In ten years, I graduated with a bachelor's degree in psychology.

There's not a lot you can do with a bachelor's degree in psychology, so I went to work for my father at the John Deere dealership. Exhausted from trying to get my dad's approval, I quit and went to work for a wholesale window treatment supplier as the office manager. I was good at it, but that wasn't my calling. I wanted to be a therapist. I've been in and out of therapy all my life. I've been around great therapists and some of the finest mental institutions in the country. I've also been to some deplorable institutions. I wanted to help people. About the time I took the job at the window treatment company, I met Debbie, my girlfriend who encouraged me to go to graduate school. I was afraid to take the graduate school entrance exam but somehow I was able to get in without having to take the exam. Again, I just keep going.

In my first year of graduate school, my field placement was at the Arkansas State Hospital, the hospital my great-uncle had run for years. I was intimidated by the severity of the patients there. One day I was walking across the campus and saw a girl sweeping the sidewalk. She had a blank look on her face: the lights were on but nobody was home. I recognized her face but couldn't quite place her. A few days later it dawned on me that she was a girl I had roomed with in the institution in North Carolina years ago. One day I asked her if her name was Sara and she said yes. I told her who I was, but she couldn't put it all together. The dramatic shift from a former roommate to an intern therapist was too much for her mind to put together. She shook her head and said she doesn't remember. It was a sad moment for me, for I had moved on but she was still on the battle ground fighting.

My second placement was at the police department, in Victim Assistance Program. This was during the last year of graduate school. I was successful there. I did a good job and they liked me. When I got out of graduate school they rehired me and fired my supervisor. I was the new boss. My life was finally beginning to turn around and I was beginning to become more self-confident. I had the degree, a good job, a husband, and a child. It was the beginnings of the American dream. Underneath it all, I was still struggling with shame because of history. To make up for it, I developed an exaggerated ego. I would have preferred humility but that's not how my internal system operated at that time. Inflated ego can be deadly and it got me in a lot of trouble. To this day when I say the Lord's Prayer, I always say, "Deliver me from the Ego," not deliver me from the evil.

My next success was landing the job with the startup of the Charter Hospital and being invited to be on the NBC Today Show, a national television show. As far as I was concerned, I had arrived! Can you imagine how happy I was to be finally seen in a positive light? It was the kind of change I was not used to. I was treated like a celebrity and was on many radio shows and in magazines. I was important, for goodness sake! It all went into my head. Low self-esteem and major successes are not good partners.

After leaving my work with the Charter Hospital, I moved to northwest Arkansas and went into private practice. It was very successful for several years until my marital problems became intense. My husband's drug abuse was at the root of it. While working together as therapists providing couples counseling, Dale couldn't stay awake. I noticed he kept dozing off during sessions. I felt sorry for him because I thought he pushing himself too hard, working long hours to take care of our family and wasn't getting enough sleep. Later I learned that the dozing off was actually an "opiate nod." It was the side effect of his prescription drug abuse. While I was familiar with alcohol abuse personally and professionally, I had no experience with the abuse of opiate prescription drug, which has become a national epidemic. The level of denial, dishonesty, and deceit often characteristic of prescription drug abusers is baffling to those of us who are not. My ex-husband's challenges—being sociopathic, alcoholic, and a drug addict—almost took me down. But I rose again, like the proverbial cat with nine lives.

When I went on the run from him with the kids to California, I was advised by my therapist not to practice therapy for a year, to just spend that time working on me. It ended up taking me three years to recover before getting my license in California to practice again. Those three years were hard for me. All the ways I had formerly defined myself no longer applied. Nobody

Expect a Miracle

in Southern California cared what family I came from, whose daughter or sister I was. I was no longer my husband's wife and I wasn't a therapist anymore. The first two times I took the California licensing exam for therapists, I failed the oral part of exam. I had no idea who I was anymore or how to "find myself." Later I saw a quote that said: "Life is not about finding yourself but about creating yourself." In retrospect, I see this was when I really began to recreate myself.

As I began to recreate myself and discover my own truths, I was ready to start serving with humility, despite my past accomplishments and successes. They no longer went to my head and I learned to give credit to Source. I began to understand my place as an instrument in God's universe. Once again I started over, but this time with a knowing that I am a spiritual being. I knew I had to put myself out there again in the world. I had developed a social phobia when I moved to California and would barely leave my house except to go to AA or to take the kids to school. I was terrified of the freeway and terrified of people. I knew that if I gave in to the phobia, it would cripple my family. So, I had to start taking risks. There is a quote in Louise Erdrich's book The Painted Drum that comes to mind: "Life will break you. Nobody can protect you from that, and living alone won't either, for solitude will also break you with its yearning. You have to love. You have to feel. It is the reason you are here on earth. You are here to risk your heart. You are here to be swallowed up. And when it happens that you are broken, or betrayed, or left, or hurt, or death brushes near, let yourself sit by an apple tree and listen to the apples falling all around you in heaps, wasting their sweetness. Tell yourself you tasted as many as you could."

Moving to California with two young children and not knowing anybody there that well was a huge risk for me. The cost of living there was much higher and I didn't know how I would make it. I had been advised that in order for us to be safe from the children's father, I needed to leave the country and lose my identity. That process involved more than I was capable of at the time. In addition, I still wasn't convinced I didn't have AIDS, so California seemed the best place. If for nothing else, treatment for AIDS was more advanced in California at the time. I had always resonated with California because the people there seemed more open and conscious than what I was used to in Arkansas. The willingness to make this move and the empowerment I received from taking the chance was well worth the risk.

My first job in California was as the clinical director of a homeless shelter for women with children. I loved the position, my staff, and my clients. I put my heart into it. But as time went on, I observed that the director of the organization was abusive, not only to me and my staff but also to our clients. My attempts to correct the situation, even involving the board of directors, were in vain. I felt that if I remained in that position, I would be covertly enabling the abuse, so I resigned. It was a hard decision to make because my family needed the income. I didn't know that this would be the first of many agencies I would leave due to unacceptable ethical standards.

Expect a Miracle

My personal history taught me the value of my ethics. Unable to find an accepted position, I felt defeated. I didn't know what to do or where to turn, so I started flooding the market with resumes. I was asked by one of the companies to interview as a program manager for a treatment program with adolescent sex offenders. I didn't send my resume for that position and was almost insulted that they were recruiting me. I discussed it with a close friend and decided it might be "God calling" and chose to go to the interview. I explained to the interviewer that I did not believe in rehabilitation for sex offenders and thought they ought to all have their abusive parts cut off. I guess she was desperate to find someone. She made me a generous offer that I couldn't refuse. I took the job. The lack of faith I had in the rehabilitation process for these kids was rooted in the unhealed sex abuse victim in me. Working with these kids facilitated my healing and forgiveness on all levels. I am so thankful I accepted God's call.

After we had lived in California for several years my daughter suggested we move somewhere where we could have more for less. I was amazed by the wisdom of this elementary school kid. I agreed. About the same time my elderly parents' health started to deteriorate. My father warned that he didn't think he and my mother could come visit us anymore. My parents had taken up the role of my kids' absent father. I started researching possible locations for us in Arkansas.

My son had been diagnosed with an autism spectrum disorder and for the first time was doing really well in the private school he attended. I had left northwest Arkansas in an awkward and shameful manner and I was scared to go back. When I left, we were the talk of the town. My ex-husband, Dale, had been fired from the University of Arkansas for forging a prescription and leaving the prescription on the copier machine at work. He and I had both relapsed. I got a DUI. He went back to rehabilitation. We were the subject of much gossip and ridicule because of our professional positions in the recovery community. So, it was really embarrassing. In spite of all that, we bravely returned to Arkansas, a town very close to our former community.

We found a school in Eureka Springs, Arkansas, that professed to understand Clay's disorder and would be able to help, so we moved to this town. Interestingly, the old hotel that is the hallmark of the town was built by my great-great-uncle, the first carpetbagger governor of Arkansas. Immediately upon enrollment at the school my son began to be bullied and the teachers and principal turned a blind eye. I ended up having to report the teacher for child abuse of another child because I was a mandated reporter. She was proven guilty and put on the child abuse registry. I began to study cults and saw that this school had all the earmarks of an educational cult. The school insisted I meet with a member of their board of directors for mediation.

Eventually my kids were asked to leave the school. My daughter went into the public school and I homeschooled my son. We were shunned by the town and couldn't get out of there fast enough. I had opened up a private practice and many of my old clients began to make the hour-long drive over to see me there. Actually my whole practice was built on clients from that town so I decided it was time to swallow my pride and move back, and I did. It turned out to be good for us and it was there I began to take the risk of dating a man and loving again.

Putting an ad in the personals, meeting, dating, and marrying Bill has taken more of me than I ever thought I had and the benefits have been worth it. Once again, I refused to believe myself incapable of a committed, successful, loving relationship, although for many years I wondered. In 2009 and 2010 my husband and I had many problems in our marriage, mostly relating to our children. We struggled as a couple and separated several times. The children were trying to divide us and they almost succeeded. In December of 2010 we had a family meeting to clear the air of all misconceptions and decided to renew our wedding vows and start anew. Neither one of us are quitters.

We decided to come to Kauai, a dream vacation spot of mine for many years, to renew our vows. For one reason or another I had always denied myself the opportunity to visit Kauai. I told myself it was too expensive, the flight was too far, and other rationalizations for not pursuing my dreams. I am so glad I didn't give up because what a magical experience it was for both of us the first ten days we visited here, so much so that we decided to move here.

Just to give you a few highlights of our visit here: We got here at dark, so we couldn't see the beauty of the island. We checked in to what turned out to be one of the fanciest hotels on the island, the St. Regis, or the St. Ritzy, as we call it. We were treated like royalty. When the sun rose and we looked out we saw we were truly in paradise. I went out to the bluff to look at the ocean and was greeted by three whales, scores of dolphins, and a double rainbow, the first of many signs to follow that we were home.

After a night or two in the hotel, we decided we wanted to move. We were tired of the snobbery of the guests, the $30 breakfasts, and the fact that we had to call a bellboy for ice and the bell captain to retrieve our car. With the luxury we lost our independence. We found a nice, chill accommodation farther north in Hanalei and were shocked and pleased when the tour company let us out of our contract and were able to move. The new place was a unit in a home a block from the beach. It was full of character. The unit next door had the pole in it that the manager told us Demi Moore used to train for her part in the movie Striptease.

My friend connected us with a kahuna (a Hawai'ian holy man) to renew our vows. We called him, set the date, and he said he would call us the day before to advise us of the location due to weather conditions. He decided to perform the service at Moloa'a Beach, which we later learned was the site for the filming of the pilot of the popular TV show when we were growing up, Gilligan's Island. So here we were, the professor and Marianne on our three-hour tour! Kel Ho, the kahuna, and his wife, Kathy, the photographer, met us and we followed them to the site. It was a lovely sacred service. Bill and I both cried all the way through it and agreed that the Hawai'ian ceremony is the only way people should ever marry. After the service we noticed hundreds of sea turtles swimming in the bay. Sea turtles represent longevity, as they lived through the age of the dinosaurs, and in Chinese myth they represent wisdom. Leaving the beach I texted my friends and families that we were now recommitted and my brother pointed out the obvious that we had overlooked: Hookers and Ho's in Hawaii! We laughed and laughed. At lunch after the service we were greeted by a pair of doves: birds, as Bill pointed out, that mate for life.

There were many more miracles and synchronistic events that happened here and we knew when we left that we wanted to return here. Our plan was to split our time between Kauai and our retreat center in northwest Arkansas, but so far Kauai has had other plans for us. She has been very welcoming to us and has made it possible for us to stay here and thrive and make a difference in other people's lives here. Our marriage and love for each other has soared to new heights and we have achieved the unconditional love of our dreams. We have many friends and angels here who have paved the way. Milan Kocek, a precious Czechoslovakian man, was our first landlord and was fast to become our friend. He did so much for us, from finding us wheels and furniture to washing our cars. Eva Hoopi sold us our land and advised us on behavior that would help us be accepted. White people here are known as haoles and are often discriminated against by the locals. She has helped us fit in and has become a friend. Through the purchase of our beloved horse, Sushi, we became friends with Katja and Greg, and through our purchases of lovely local art we found our first Southern friends,

Amy-Lauren and Camille. The local health food store brings me a source of comfort and support every time I go in through their warm-hearted and humble cashier, Debbie. I have yet to connect with my father's past girlfriend, Betty Claire Greenlea Carroll, but I really look forward to meeting her and hearing her stories. The workshop on publishing I went to here connected me with my editor Zeal, and offering a tent site to a young lady brought friendship with Caitlin and many young people on the island. An ad I put on Craigslist looking for people to help on our farm got the attention of a department head at Kauai Community College and he invited us to take part in a consortium of local farmers to help Kauai achieve sustainability.

I recently got accepted into the Kauai Community College Culinary Arts program. When I was in the halfway house at the mental institution at age eighteen, I signed up at the local community college to be a chef, but the program required the kind of physical abilities I didn't possess at the time. I was obese. In the halfway house, you either had to have a job, do volunteer work, be a day patient, which meant taking part in programs at the hospital, or go to school. I didn't want to do any more of the programs. I had done all the ceramics, weaving, pottery, and group therapy that I ever wanted to do. But I was so institutionalized that I could not function in a school for "normies" yet. I certainly couldn't get and hold a job for any length of time. For over thirty years since then, I have wanted to become a chef and was off and on looking at different schools for possibilities of classes that I could take. It didn't work out until now, but I never gave up.

Expect a Miracle

Moving to Kauai was a huge risk, and fortunately I've learned all the benefits that come from taking risks. The more risks you take, the better you feel about yourself, because you are trusting Source to take care of you. I'm not talking about going and jumping off that cliff without something on my back, but calculated risks. As Joseph Campbell says, "Follow your bliss."

While I say never give up or surrender, letting go can also be productive. There are times to give up on a relationship that is abusive or not working anymore, but only the individual involved can know that. I don't ever pretend to know what is best for someone else. I was working with a victim of domestic violence when I worked at the police department in Colorado. At that time, I held the belief that all victims of domestic violence need to get out and get out now. This client left her partner and he killed her. She might have been alive today if she had stayed; I don't know. I think each person has the answers within them and if their intuition tells them it's time to go, then it's time to go. To me that is surrender, not giving up. In Hawaiian, it's known as holo holo, which means going with the flow, not forcing yourself, not pushing doors open, but just seeing if they're open, being open, accepting, and being receptive. I have a hard enough time knowing what is right for me. I released my first husband after doing all I could to make the marriage and family work. It is hard for parents with young children to make the decision to divorce, because of the potential impact on the children. I learned that the children do better when the primary caregiver is happy, with as little stress as possible. Staying together for the sake of the kids seldom works.

There are times you have to let your kids go. And I don't mean give up on them, but you let go of them. If you can't help them for fun and for free when they are adults, you don't need to be helping them. An old sponsor in AA shared that wisdom with me. In other words, if you can't do things for your kids willingly, without expectations, then don't. I'm going through that right now with my twenty-year-old daughter. Trusting that she has her own path and her own way, I'm there for emotional support but that's all. She and her brother began to see me as an ATM machine. I withdrew because I want them to be able to survive if I'm not around anymore.

There are times to surrender and there are times to just keep going. I have to live inwardly to know when the right time is. Surrender itself is a part of the never giving up. If I didn't surrender my relationship with my ex-husband, I wouldn't have been able to continue my personal journey.

Right when I had breast cancer, I was driving down the road, listening to a breast cancer expert on the radio. She was talking about recovering from breast cancer and suggested that listeners ask themselves, "Do people tire me or do they inspire me?" I don't hang around people who tire me anymore. I only hang around people who inspire me.

Another important lesson I learned as I look back is that my gut never lied to me. My parents would tell me not to judge a book by its cover. "You're judging them too fast," they would say whenever I decided to move on from a relationship. But it wasn't judgment. It wasn't in my head. I knew these people weren't right for me. I taught that to my kids, to follow their gut instinct.

Above all, the most important lesson I learned was the importance of meditation. I learned to get really still and quiet, to discern. We as humans can make anything appear like God's will to us if we want it badly enough. We can have such intense desires that we can create "signs" to support and validate our wishes and desires. But that can backfire on us. To get really still and quiet and discern between my higher self and my lower self has been a valuable experience. It is the difference between what your mind is telling you and what is really coming from deep within. The mind is a master of illusions. It's very tricky and can play a lot of games on you; a way around that is learning how to meditate and meditating regularly.

Twelve

Acknowledging My Angels

"At times our own light goes out and is rekindled by a spark from another person. Each of us has cause to think with deep gratitude of those who have lighted the flame within us."

— Albert Schweitzer

As I reflect on my journey, I am hit full flush on the face by the many people that the universe had lined up to make sure that I did not waste away. In all humility, I feel kind of special that nature thought so highly of me that it decided to spare me. In addition to my husband, Bill, many people were relentless to see that I made it. And as I look back, there was really nothing in it for them. Yes, the shrinks made money for treating me, but some of them went way beyond the call of duty to do it. And I'm sure they didn't get paid for many of the things they did. Then there were nurses, friends, and strangers who came forth at different times to help, most of them having no idea how important they were in the course of my journey. Some of them were soft-hearted and kind. Some were tough with me. Some let me go because they knew that was the best thing for me. They were all my angels and I'm so very grateful. I suppose that they did what they did, because at some level, they refused to give up on me. Can you imagine how blown away and fulfilled my "angels" must have felt when they learned years later that I had earned a master's degree and become a counselor? Such an accomplishment would have been inconceivable in the mind of any normal person who had met me at age sixteen.

Susan Hickman was a nurse on the first psych ward I went to in Little Rock. While I was outwardly rebellious, I was inwardly terrified and alone. Susan saw me and loved me unconditionally, going way beyond what was expected of her as a nurse. She became a good friend and we are still in contact.

"Lunch Queen," as I nicknamed her, was my favorite nurse at Highland Hospital in North Carolina and interestingly shares her birthday with Susan. She was married to the administrator of the hospital. I always liked it when she was on duty and I looked forward to seeing her. I admired her so much that I wrote her a poem about how much I appreciated her, adapted it to a counted cross-stitch sampler, and framed it for her. She was moved. She missed work a lot for some odd reason. I was always devastated when she didn't show up. I kept in touch with her and still do. Come to find out, her husband was having an affair, and she started drinking and having problems. She went to AA and pretty much feels the same way about it now as I do. I think I might have died if it weren't for her love. She saw me for who I really was. My daughter got her middle name from her.

Dr. Bonner, my shrink, was a dedicated angel. He saw me through a lot. He was the first one I confided to about my incest. He was always there if I needed anything and would not tolerate it if a staff member was mean to me. He was my lifelong therapist who never gave up on me.

You didn't meet my first boyfriend, Lee. He was the cousin of one of my best friends and was sent by his parents from England to Arkansas to live with his grandmother when he got in trouble. He was a character and I loved him so, hanging out with him when I was home in between hospitalizations. He was sweet and kind to me, yet another tortured soul who later killed himself.

I never mentioned my award-winning boyfriend, Tommy, my second serious boyfriend. Well, when I was sixteen, I traveled to Myrtle Beach, California with him just to hang out. After spending our first night there, we went to the beach the next day. We seemed to be having lots of fun. Then he came up to me and said that he was hungry and was going to get us some food. I said, "Sure." I waited and waited for him to come back with the food but he never did. In fact, I never saw him again, ever! I went back to the hotel and there was a note on the desk that said, "Dear lady, I am leaving for your own good. Here's some money for your trip back. Stay and enjoy yourself.

Expect a Miracle

Love, Tommy." I stood there holding the note in my hand and wondering where I went wrong with this guy. I'm thinking, "If you wanted to break up, why be so dramatic?" There I was in a hotel room, seven hours away, sixteen years old, and didn't know anyone. I called my doctor and my parents and didn't know how to explain the situation. My angel doctor, Dr. Bonner, kicked in again, helped arrange to get me back to North Carolina, and when I arrived at midnight, he was waiting for me in his office. He didn't have to do that. He went way above and beyond the call of duty for me. I really appreciated that. Many years later I learned that Tommy committed suicide.

The Westbrook family was my adopted family. When I was a teenager, Mitzie and George Westbrook were like my parents. Mitzie and I are similar in that we don't hide our feelings. We tell it like it is, unlike in my family, where everybody pretends. Every day after school, I'd go and sleep off my medications at the Westbrooks' home. They'd feed me dinner before I went home. Their daughter Debra was my best friend. I missed them when they moved to Dyersburg, Tennessee, but had opportunities to spend some time with them when I was driving back and forth from Highland Hospital in Asheville, North Carolina to Arkansas. I'd stop and spend the night with them on the way because it was too far of a drive and I really needed a break. Mitzie and George and their daughters have been lifelong friends and Robin, the youngest daughter, is one of my closest friends today.

Steve "D." was an ob-gyn in recovery. The impaired

professionals committee had gone after him for drinking too much chardonnay. He had three kids and was a good father. My ex-husband, Dale, became friends with him, and each time Dale took our kids to go hang out with him, Steve would end up taking care of my kids. After Dale left California and moved to Texas to get married, Steve remained friends with my family and was a father figure for my children for a while. He bought them elaborate gifts for their birthdays. He even took my daughter to her first father-daughter dance in grade school. He stood in as my kids' father whenever the occasion called for it and was a good friend to me.

When I first went to rehab in California and was told that I needed to get rid of Dale to get my life back, there was a lady named Pat who was a patient with me at the rehab center. She lived in this exclusive part of town called La Jolla. She didn't even know me but she gave me and the kids a place to stay until I could find our own place. There were always angels to shelter me from the storm.

Then there was my girlfriend Debbie, who loved me unconditionally and encouraged me to apply to graduate school. She believed in me when I didn't believe in myself. I wouldn't have gone to graduate school and been able to help so many people without her encouragement.

You have read about our family Methodist minister, Brother Ed, throughout these pages. He and his precious wife, Pat, have been friends of my family for over forty years. They have married, buried, and baptized pretty much the whole extended family. They have been a source of strength, support, encouragement, and humor for me my whole life and I love and appreciate them sincerely.

In graduate school I had two professors who profoundly shaped my career as a professional: Ruth Parsons and Pam Metz. Pam helped me reconcile my issues with my sexuality. She guided me to not merely accept myself and my history but embrace them. She taught me that while I had a story, I was not my story. Ruth came from the same area of eastern Kentucky as my grandmother. She was a strong, bright woman, full of character. She was and is a role model for my professional life. She cautioned me about the risks of being honest, candid, and straightforward, stating that people would either love me or hate me and that I would often be seen as a messiah or a pariah; I was neither.

I mentioned Mary Roush, my therapist and mentor, when I talked about opening my private practice. Mary provided much love and guidance to me as her client and then as I became a therapist and mother. My daughter got her first name from Mary.

For many years my two best friends were a gay couple, Sam and John. Sam was psychic and open and John was loyal and grounded. They both helped me in ways too numerous to mention. A whole book could be written about the times we have shared. I wouldn't have been the person or the mother I was without them. They saved my butt on more occasions than anyone.

Ilona Lifshultz was my body worker who became my friend when I lived in Southern California. She not only helped heal my children and me, she opened my eyes to healthy eating, alternative healing, and the spiritual and metaphysical worlds. She and I are connected on many levels. She strongly suggested that Bill and I come to Kauai when we decided to renew our vows. Without her loving guidance, we would have had a hard time finding our way home to Kauai.

My last girlfriend, Louise, taught me how to open my heart. I learned to love by loving her. I remember late one night standing in her kitchen arguing and I wanted to quit and go to bed. She told me that if I wanted to be in a relationship with a woman I had to have the will to process through to the end, because only men drop it and go to bed. Later, when she broke up with me, she very lovingly told me that she only goes to the movie, that I am the movie.

And last but not least, my publisher and healer, Dr. Zeal Okogeri. It was in his workshop that I realized I could write this book. His patience and perseverance have ensured that my dream of writing this book became a reality. He is from Nigeria and has traveled extensively. His international perspective has helped me tremendously. He is a teacher of the Light and Sound Current meditation and an incredible healer in the art of Letting Go. He has guided and helped me "let go" of much of my history and concerns about the future.

Expect a Miracle

Space would not permit, but I would have loved to give each person full credit for their contribution to my life. And if there's any "angel" whose name is left out of the pages of this book, I want him or her to know that his or her name is not left out of my heart. I am very grateful to all of you! Many have been mentioned throughout the book and many have not. To all my clients through the years, you have been my greatest angels. Having the privilege of watching you do your work is why I went into the career I did and I feel honored to have been a part of your journey.

To all who have criticized me, hated me, put me down, I say thank you for giving me the impetus to better myself and move forward. Like the Chinese proverb says: Fall down seven times, get up eight.

And a special thank you to those of you who are reading these words for being a part of my journey. I sure hope all this craziness somehow enriches your life. I invite you to stay in touch through my website, www.askahooker.us

As we say in Hawaiian, *Mahalo!*

Expect a Miracle

Sources

Hare, Dr. Robert *Without Conscience: The Disturbing World of the Psychopaths Among Us.*

Dryden-Edwards, Roxanne MD; Stöppler, Melissa Conrad MD. *Schizophrenia*

Andrews, Ted. *Animal Speak*

Meloy, Reid PhD. *The Psychopathic Mind*

Stout, Martha. *The Sociopath Next Door*

Erdrich, Louise. *The Painted Drum*

Credits

Front and back cover photos by Danny Hashimoto

Hair by Linda Oshima at Plaza Hair Kapaʻa

Necklace by Katja Langholz of Mineral Amorphia Kapaʻa

Tropical clothing from Tropical Tantrum Kapaʻa

EXPECT A MIRACLE

FOR MORE INFORMATION,
please contact:
Marianne Jones Hooker

www.askahooker.us

CPSIA information can be obtained at www.ICGtesting.com
Printed in the USA
LVOW062101290212

270978LV00001B/231/P